AN ANTIQUE MURDER

An absolutely gripping murder mystery full of twists

NORMAN RUSSELL

An Oldminster Mystery Book 2

JOFFE
BOOKS

Joffe Books, London
www.joffebooks.com

First published in Great Britain in 2022

Cover art by Dee Dee Book Covers

ISBN: 978-1-80405-094-1

PROLOGUE

Flight from Stutthof, 13 February 1945

The long, winding procession of prisoners and their SS guards trudged through the snowy wastes of marshland and stunted forest on the forced march that would take them from the concentration camp at Stutthof to the embarkation docks at Danzig on the Baltic Sea coast. It was bitterly cold, with an east wind blowing, but most of the five hundred prisoners had long ceased to feel anything but a kind of numbed fatality. They were the victims of the Third Reich and would die as such, robbed of their names, their humanity, their possessions, and of all hope. They would march for twenty miles until they reached the city. Those who fell by the wayside through illness, malnutrition and exhaustion would be summarily shot in the head, and left to lie in the snow, where the wolves would later find them.

Five hundred men and women clad in thin pyjama suits and caps, stretching into the dim distance. They could hear the thundering of the Russian heavy artillery from the east as the Red Army approached. Adolf Hitler's stranglehold on the land was finally beginning to loosen — and everyone knew it. Ten miles on, and they began to encounter lines of

German people fleeing from Danzig in a desperate attempt to reach those parts of Germany not yet occupied by the Allied forces. These people knew that the Russian soldiers would exact terrible vengeance for the years of war.

One man in the convoy of civilians had determined that he was not going to perish in the coming Armageddon. When the time was ripe, he would simply slip away, probably as they dragged themselves through a small town or village. He had a map, and one precious document that would almost guarantee his survival. Yesterday had been his twenty-first birthday, his coming of age. Well, it was also going to be the birth of a new life for him, away from the horrors of Stutthof. The Third Reich was doomed, and a new era beckoned. His friend Klaus Heinemann — if you could have a friend in a hellhole like Stutthof — planned to lose himself among the crowds in Danzig itself, and then stow away on one of the Baltic ships and so get to Norway, but he had other ideas.

They trudged through a populous village seven miles to the south of Danzig as night was falling, and the young man contrived to slip away from the column down a side road that led him across a cemetery and out into a belt of farmland. He could see the red glow of fires kindled by incendiary bombs that had rained down on the great Baltic city. The past was over and done with. It was now time to make his way resolutely to the West.

1. HUSBANDS AND WIVES

Detective Sergeant Glyn Edwards retrieved his key from his overcoat pocket and let himself in to his narrow terrace house in Hood Street, a stone's throw from Oldminster station. A few letters lay in the hall, and he bent to put them on the hall stand beside his briefcase.

'Hello, Sandra — I'm home!'

There had been a time when his wife would have greeted him with a kiss and a stream of questions about what kind of day he'd had, and whether he and the guvnor had bagged any criminals. But that had been when they were both in their twenties, and Sandra had been expecting. They had been both lovers and comrades, spending what free time they had on renovating the house, neglected for years by the previous owner, so that they were constantly surrounded by tins of paint and rolls of wallpaper. He'd still been a uniformed constable then; it was only after he'd turned thirty that he had passed the necessary examinations to become a detective, which meant, among other things, the luxury of going into plain clothes.

But now there was no answer to his greeting. The house was cold and cheerless. He went into the living room. There were magazines lying on the floor near the couch, and a half-consumed box of chocolates stood open on the coffee table. He glanced at his reflection in the mirror over the fireplace. Gaunt, hatchet-faced, tired. Did he really look that old? He was only thirty-eight, and in good health. No, it was not work that was turning him into an old man before his time. Work gave purpose to his life, a sense of fulfilment and self-worth. But here, in this cold, empty house, he felt his spirits crushed. What had been their home — his and Sandra's — had become a prison for both of them. Closing the front door was like snapping shut the gate of a cage.

There was a note for him, propped up against the clock.

Have gone to Pilates at the Institute. Back about nine. Your dinner's in the oven.

He went into the kitchen and retrieved the shepherd's pie, which was on the point of being overcooked. A little line of gravy bubbled over the edge of the foil basin. He turned it out on to a plate and got a can of beer from the fridge.

As he sat down, his mind returned to the letters in the hallway. The postman came at two o'clock or thereabouts. Why had they still been lying unretrieved on the floor? Perhaps Sandra just couldn't be bothered. She'd have stepped over them to get out of the front door on her way to the institute. She was just as much a prisoner in the house as he was. More, perhaps, once she'd quit her job. He'd thought that she'd loved being a floor manager at Robson's in Oldminster — she'd had so many stories to tell him about the customers and the staff. But that was back in the old days, when they'd been happy.

When he had finished his dinner, he went out into the back yard for a smoke. Sandra had always complained of his smoking, and so did the guvnor, but it was a habit he had yet to break. It brought him peace: sometimes, in the winter, he'd stand there smoking, and looking up at the stars.

He was catching up on some work when, just before nine, he heard Sandra's key in the lock, and then she called out: 'I'm home!'

They were the same age, and Sandra had never lost her allure. She was as slim and attractive as she had been in her twenties, her pale complexion set off by her luxuriant black hair.

Glyn knew they stayed together because neither of them had anywhere else to go.

'How did you get on today?' she asked.

'Everything was fine. How was Pilates?'

'Fine.'

'Have you had anything to eat?'

'I'll make myself a sandwich in a minute.'

She sat down on the couch and picked up the *Radio Times*.

'I think there's a Hugh Grant film on at ten,' she said. 'Let's see. Yes, there it is.'

'Right,' Glyn murmured, then before he could stop himself: 'Why didn't you pick up the mail off the hall floor?'

'Well, I could see it was only junk mail. And in any case, you did it, so why make a fuss?'

'Making a fuss' was to make a simple request that other people wouldn't think twice about granting: 'This food's cold. Didn't you turn the oven up high enough?' 'Oh, Glyn, don't make such a fuss.' 'That stove could do with a clean.' 'Oh, Glyn, don't make such a fuss. I'll do it later.' He wouldn't 'make a fuss' — had never thought of himself as that kind of a person — but she had said when she'd stopped working that it was to spend more time working on the house. Finishing the DIY, getting things 'right'. All the things he was too tired to do after a punishing day on the job. But she wasn't doing any of that, and Glyn did most of the cleaning even though he worked full-time.

Glyn Edwards was a native of Oldminster, but Sandra came from Southbourne, on the coast. Her widowed mother still lived there, and for the past two years or so Sandra had been paying her longer and longer visits. Her mother was supposedly suffering from various illnesses that required her daughter's presence. At first, he'd felt resentful about these visits, but with time, he began to see them as a kind of relief. When Sandra wasn't there, he could breathe more freely.

'Glyn?'

'What?'

'I really think I should go and see my mum again. She's really not well, and somehow when I'm with her she seems to perk up. It'll only be for a week or two. You can manage here, can't you?'

'Oh, yes. Go by all means. I'll be all right here.'

Sandra got up from the couch and gave him a perfunctory hug.

'Thanks. I'll make myself that sandwich now.'

Glyn watched his wife as she stood at the kitchen table, busying herself with a packet of sliced ham and a couple of tomatoes. She worked mechanically, and he could see that her mind was elsewhere. There was an expression on her face that he couldn't fathom, a sort of dreamy smile of anticipation. He suddenly felt a chill grip his stomach. All these visits to her mother — were they something more than that? No, nonsense. She was just bored, and trapped, as he was.

Sandra had suffered a miscarriage three years earlier, and the doctors had told her that she could not have children. It had been devastating for both of them, and their marriage had gone downhill since then. They merely became used to each other, so that the marriage tie had become a strangling ligature. Once, they had holidayed together every year, but in the end that had stopped, with Sandra preferring to visit her mother at the seaside. He endured this life because there was no alternative. Sandra had suffered considerably from being denied motherhood, and it was his duty to stick with her, as she did with him. But now that secret little smile of triumph niggled. What was she up to?

* * *

'Moira! I'm home.'

As Detective Inspector Paul French stepped into the hall his wife came out of the kitchen to greet him. She was wiping her hands on a kitchen cloth. It always came as a delightful shock of surprise to Paul that this lovely woman of thirty-two had ever consented to marry him, a rather prim policeman in his late forties. To the amusement of everyone they knew, they had met at a stuffy old bridge club, and found that they were both fanatical adherents of the game. That had helped, but it was their mutual attraction as a man and woman that had set them on the road to courtship and marriage. And then, last year, Moira had given birth to their baby daughter, whom they had called Betty.

At just a year old, Betty had already established an ascendancy over her doting father. Moira was often amused to hear her strait-laced husband talking baby language to his daughter, and to see him playing peek-a-boo with her, a game which invariably ended in the two of them giggling as Betty commandeered his glasses to play with.

The Frenches lived in a 1930s detached house in Priory Lane, which stood just outside the cathedral precinct. Moira taught children with learning disabilities three mornings a week, and on those occasions Betty was consigned to Fluffy Bunnies, the daftly named crèche run in the basement of a house in Cathedral Green.

'How was work today, darling?' asked Moira. 'Any crimes to solve?'

'No crimes today. Just a lot of paperwork — mainly traffic matters. Where's baby?'

'Baby's in the kitchen, watching me preparing a lamb casserole for tomorrow. It's quiche and salad for dinner tonight, with a bottle of that new Pinot from Robinson's.' She turned back to the kitchen. 'How's the Lost Waif?'

'Glyn Edwards?' he asked, following his wife. 'He's fine. Well, he isn't, really. I don't think things are great for him at home. Half the time he turns up at Jubilee House without breakfast, and I'll see him gulp down a cup of tea in the canteen before coming up to report to me. It's a shame, you know. He's a first-class detective, and it's sad his home life isn't going as well as his career.'

In the kitchen, Betty was sitting in her high chair, the little tray covered with an array of rather-chewed soft toys. There were squeals of delight, and a multitude of kisses, culminating in Betty once more commandeering her father's glasses, which were soon covered in milky fingerprints.

Paul French peered myopically at his wife, as she prepared tomorrow's casserole. She was a very attractive blonde, smartly dressed with a great sense of style. He smiled as he recalled their going to see a production of Agatha Christie's *The Mousetrap* at Oldminster Playhouse, where he'd got into conversation with an elderly soldierly sort of man in the interval. The man had asked him whether his daughter was enjoying the play. 'Young people usually like something with more "edge" these days, don't they?' said the soldierly man. *His daughter!* His first reaction had been one of amusement: he knew that he contrived to look older than his years. It was amazing how the fun of their earlier days together had never left them: he would deliberately act older, passing prim judgements on various celebrities and 'personalities' until she dissolved into laughter.

Poor Glyn Edwards, he mused. He never talked about his home life, never mentioned his wife by name, and French had responded by never broaching the subject. Perhaps the couple would work something out, but he doubted it.

2. SPOILS OF WAR

In the leafy suburb of Belle Vale, generally regarded as an exclusive area in the ancient cathedral city of Oldminster, was the Irving Home for Retired Actors. It stood in two acres of grounds, and the formal gardens and lawns were bounded by a thick thorn hedge, beyond which lay a sizeable vegetable garden. Although part of the Irving Home, it was run as a kind of subsidiary business by the home's gardener, Terry Lucas.

Terry was handsome, a well-made thirty-something with a shock of curly chestnut hair. He was said to be 'one for the ladies', and he certainly had a following of his own in the town. He lived on the premises, in what had been the lodge of the house when it was a private residence. He grew a good range of vegetables and fruit, and had a wide clientele, making weekly deliveries in his white Ford van.

He stood, one day in late March, leaning on his spade, and watching a middle-aged lady with untidy blonde hair as she emerged from the house carrying a box file. He smiled ruefully to himself. *Nothing doing there.*

Cathy Billington was the secretary at the Irving Home, a widow with a steady income and something put by. She treated him to the occasional smile whenever they met, but he knew that she was no soft touch. Her money would be quite safe from any attempt he might make to wheedle it out of her.

Cathy nodded briefly as he caught her eye, and then disappeared from sight as she turned the corner of the house. *Oh, well. Never mind about Cathy.* When it came to augmenting his income, he had other very profitable irons in the fire.

* * *

There were one or two people in the bar, workers from the wholesale fruit market nearby. Sitting hunched over the bar was the massive figure of Colin Sagawa. He wore an old-fashioned trilby hat, and a long, open mackintosh, which hung down like a tent around the bar stool. He was looking a bit out of sorts, which made the crescent moon and star tattoo on his right cheek stand out in livid green and red.

Terry ordered a pint of mild and sat beside him at the bar. He slipped a wad of notes to Sagawa, who swiftly counted them, nodded, and put them in one of his mac pockets.

'Very good, very nice,' he said. For such a big man, he had a slightly squeaky voice. 'So, how's the market garden business? All going well, is it? Are you still buying stuff from Sainsbury's and passing it off as your own?' Terry just nodded in response. 'Well, it don't matter, as long as the cash customers are happy. You might like to try the schools and colleges, Terry. You've not explored that territory enough yet. The boss has made a list of contacts for you, two at the Cathedral School, and another at Oldshire University. It's a way in, Terry, a sure-fire way of expanding your business.'

He handed Terry a folded piece of paper.

'You can expect another delivery of garden requisites from Green County Traders this coming Monday,' he said. 'And you're quite happy with the way things are? No worries? No complaints?' When Terry replied that all was well, Sagawa gave a grunt of satisfaction. 'Good, that's how it should be. Finish your drink and be on your way: they'll be missing you at the Irving Home. How are the old codgers? No chance of business there, I suppose.'

'No, nothing like that. The codgers are fine, Mr Sagawa. They're all doddery, but they're a good laugh. Sir Frank Taylor gets a bit shirty at times, but he's our star resident, and after all, he is ninety-four.' He downed his drink. 'I'll be getting off, then. See you whenever.' He swung off his bar stool and headed for the gents.

He had scarcely entered the toilets when Colin Sagawa was on him, pinning him against the wall, his huge ham of a hand round his throat. The tattoo shone livid on his cheek, and his eyes had assumed that insane look that frightened so many people.

'You've been seen,' Sagawa hissed, 'talking to one of Ernie Shirtcliff's boys from London. If you've got any ideas in that direction, forget them now. Those London outfits are not for the likes of you. If you seriously try to betray us, you'll find us Birmingham folk can be very unpleasant.'

After choking him a little further, Sagawa withdrew his hand, and left the toilets. Terry slid to the floor, which was wet with disinfectant. He felt fear, yes, but his fear was over-come by a burning rage. What did he care for Sagawa, with his idle threats, or for the 'big boss'? His business had netted him over £10,000, all in cash, and when he was good and ready, he'd make his move. He was strong and ruthless in his own way. There was life for him beyond the provinces. London beckoned.

* * *

Mervyn Sanders sat behind the counter of the Old Curiosity Shop, his cluttered treasure house of antiques, curios, and *objets de vertu* situated in a little paved yard off Provost's Lane, in the shadow of Oldminster Cathedral. Business was thriv-ing, for not only was there a steady stream of sophisticated customers, but his now well-established quarterly catalogue brought requests from purchasers throughout the country.

But on this blustery day in March it was a letter from nearer home that held his interest. It came from a Mr Charles Forshaw, one of the residents in the Irving Home for Retired Actors. Could Mr Sanders call on him one day that week, to look at some items of silver and jewellery? He knew Mr Sanders by reputation, but had also been recommended to him by Lord Renfield, who, he believed, had once done business with him. Well, why not? If Mr Forshaw was available that afternoon, he'd be more than happy to call on him. It was amazing how retired folk often possessed very valuable items without realizing their worth, rather like some of those people who produced almost literally priceless items for evaluation on *Antiques Road Show*. He picked up the phone and dialled the number for the Irving Home.

'Good morning, this is the Irving Home. My name is Trudy Vosper, how can I help you?' said a rather breathless voice. He told her how she could help him, and she asked him to hold the line while she went to check if Mr Forshaw was in. There followed a series of crackling noises, and then a very precise, cultured voice said: 'Charles Forshaw here.'

Their conversation was brief. Yes, Forshaw would be home that afternoon. Would three o'clock be convenient? Good. He looked forward to seeing Mr Sanders then.

Mervyn looked round his shop with great satisfaction. There were glass display cases holding enamelled snuff boxes, Fabergé egg replicas, jewelled paper knives, clockwork music boxes, each piece unique in its own way. Perhaps this Mr Forshaw would have something of genuine interest, but he was prepared to buy quite humdrum stuff, which he was able to dispose of through another establishment of his — a closely guarded secret — a high-class pawn shop in Chichester.

The walls were covered with solemnly ticking long-case clocks and old silvered mirrors, together with a collection of antique weaponry, swords, daggers, flintlock pistols and muskets. Beside the shop door stood a rather alarming suit of Samurai armour. There were a lot of good replicas about, but all his stock was genuine, and people knew that. Mervyn Sanders was something of an expert on weaponry.

He hoped today's visit would add to the collection. Mervyn called a farewell to his assistant as he left. Young Clive was proving to be an asset, willing and anxious to please, and with a nicely developing taste under Mervyn's tutelage. It was time to see what Charles Forshaw had to offer.

* * *

As Mervyn parked his car at the front entrance of the Irving Home, he noted that a young gardener had stopped work to admire the vehicle. Well, so he might. Not many people possessed a maroon Bentley. Although it was second-hand, or 'pre-loved' as the dealer had put it, the vehicle had cost him a small fortune.

He caught sight of himself in the mirror and stopped smiling. Not a very prepossessing sight, he had to admit: balding head, round face, double chin, and slightly protruding ears, which had earned him the nickname 'Dumbo' at school. But his piercing blue eyes — well, they held all the shrewdness of a connoisseur and businessman. He liked to think they were eyes that could, if the situation required it, look into another man's soul . . .

He was received at the Irving Home by a nurse, who led him along a carpeted corridor to a door marked 'Room 1'. She knocked, and the door was opened by a handsome, upright elderly man with a full head of hair and a rather attractive haggard smile.

'Come in, Mr Sanders,' he said. 'I'm Charles Forshaw. It's very good of you to come so soon. Would you care for a glass of sherry?'

This is more like it, Mervyn thought. All very civilized. Charles Forshaw brought them sherry, and they sat down facing each other in two armchairs drawn up to the electric fire.

'I'm sure I've met you somewhere before, Mr Forshaw,' said Mervyn. 'Could it have been at Eastbourne?'

Charles Forshaw laughed. 'It could well have been anywhere, Mr Sanders. You may have seen me on television years and years ago. People often think that they've seen me in real life.'

'Well, that's very interesting!' Mervyn laughed. 'And you want to show me some pieces that you think I might buy?'

At this, Charles Forshaw blushed — for reasons not lost on Mervyn. The man clearly wanted to raise money without seeming to be in need of it. He smiled encouragement, and Forshaw took him across the room to a table standing beneath the window. Oh, yes! There were indeed some nice things here. A pair of Georgian candlesticks, two snuff boxes inlaid with mother-of-pearl . . . all mid-eighteenth century. A Victorian diamond brooch. Forshaw respected his silence as he closely examined all the pieces through a hand lens. Then he stood back.

'Some very nice things, there, Mr Forshaw. I can give you £2,500 for them. Would that be acceptable?'

'It most certainly would! I'd no idea that they'd fetch that. None of these things have any sentimental value, you know. I just acquired them as little investments during my acting years.'

'People very often own things that are far more valuable than they thought,' said Mervyn Sanders. 'They—'

He suddenly stopped, his whole body tense. He almost staggered and was obliged to steady himself by placing a hand on the wall.

'Mr Sanders, what's the matter?' Charles asked, sounding worried. 'You've gone quite pale. Are you ill?'

'No, no . . . It's that dagger on the windowsill. Is that part of what you want to sell? May I sit down for a moment? And could you fetch me a glass of water?'

Charles Forshaw hurried into his en suite bathroom and came back with the water. Taking some deep breaths, Mervyn straightened up and reached for the dagger.

'Oh, *that*,' said Charles Forshaw. 'It's supposed to be a Nazi dagger, but I expect it's a replica. But it isn't mine. You see, Mr Sanders, there are things in this house that tend to go walkabout. A bit like kleptomania, you know. What's yours is mine. That kind of thing.'

Mervyn had recovered his equanimity. He put the dagger on the table, and sat down again before looking back at Forshaw. He had no idea what the older man was talking about. *Kleptomania?*

It was only when Forshaw spoke again that Mervyn was enlightened.

'Ah! I see what you mean. Yes, I quite understand. And are you going to tell me who actually owns this dagger? You can tell him that I'll give him £300 for it . . .'

Twenty minutes later, Mervyn was ready to go with his newly acquired artefacts. He turned to leave, but there was something very honest and open about Charles Forshaw that made him pause on the threshold.

'Mr Forshaw,' he said, 'you saw that I almost fainted when I saw that Nazi dagger on your windowsill. I'm Jewish. My family are of Hungarian descent, and during the war they suffered terribly under the Nazis and their collaborators. Both sides of my family, numbering twenty-four men, women and children, died in the gas chambers. My parents—' He broke off. 'But there, I can see I've made you uncomfortable. But I think you'll understand that seeing these mementoes of the Third Reich close up can trigger some *difficult* feelings.'

'My dear fellow,' Charles Forshaw cried, 'I can understand your horror. I can only apologize for leaving the thing there in plain sight and speaking of it so lightly.' He sighed. 'What a terrible time it was. So many decent families like your own . . .'

He didn't finish the thought, but their eyes met in shared understanding. *Gone. All gone.*

3. SO MUCH BLOOD

Mervyn had not expected to hear again from his elderly client at the Irving but not long after, he received a letter from Charles Forshaw. It was quite unexpected, but its contents seemed to him to be a gift from the gods.

> *Dear Sanders,*
>
> *I am by way of being the 'resident redcoat' here at the Irving Home for Retired Actors, charged with providing an interesting speaker once a month to come to dinner (the food's very good here) and then give a talk to us in the common room afterwards. The whole thing is over by ten o'clock or thereabouts. Could I persuade you to come and speak to us? Any evening this coming April would be fine. Our house manager here, George Cavanagh, told me that you gave a talk on medieval manuscripts to the Friends of Oldminster Cathedral last month, which was thoroughly enjoyed. Please let me know if you are able to oblige me.*
>
> *Sincerely yours,*
> *Charles Forshaw*

How nice it was to receive a proper letter on headed notepaper, and sent through the post, instead of an email! He sent a reply at once.

My dear Mr Forshaw,

I was delighted to receive your letter. I relish the idea of dining with such a distinguished assembly of British thespians and would suggest Friday 20 April. The title of my talk would be: The Homes and Haunts of the Russian Crown Jewels. The first time we met, I told you something about my background. Although Friday begins the Sabbath, I am not a strictly observant Jew, and have no special dietary requirements. I very much look forward to seeing you all on the 20th.

Sincerely yours,

Mervyn Sanders

* * *

It was ten o'clock on the evening of the 20 April, when Charles Forshaw showed Mervyn Sanders to the door of the Irving Home. The receptionist had already left for the night, but the place still looked homely and warm.

'I must thank you again, Mr Sanders, for such an interesting talk. Was that really true about the grand duchess letting you handle the imperial sceptre? And the bit about when you wore the Tsar's coronation ring?'

'Quite true, Mr Forshaw.' Mervyn beamed. 'You come across all sorts in my line of work.' He pulled the door open and shivered at the chilly air. 'These spring nights. Don't let me keep you in the cold, Mr Forshaw.'

Charles bid the other man farewell and made his way back to the common room as he heard the door clunk locked behind him. Two other inhabitants of the Irving Home for Retired Actors had not yet gone to bed. Sitting in the comfortable common room, reminiscing about old times and past performances on stage and screen, they were lingering over a glass or two of port before retiring for the night. Their most distinguished resident was in critical mood.

'Now Charles, here,' said Sir Frank Taylor, 'was never tall enough to play Macbeth. You shouldn't have done it.

That provincial tour you did with the Stratford Players in sixty-four was a disaster! You were five foot six, and Marion Forbes as Lady Macbeth was six foot tall. You were forever craning your neck to look her in the eyes!'

Charles Forshaw gave a good-humoured laugh as he sat back down in his comfortable chair. Dear old Frank! At ninety-four he was very frail, and nearly blind, but his mind and memory were still as sharp as scalpels, and his genius for getting under people's skin had not abated with age. His voice, too, was strong, though high-pitched now; the mellow, fulsome tones that had held audiences enthralled in the sixties now lacked depth and timbre. The old fellow had closed his eyes, but Charles Forshaw suspected that he was still listening to the conversation.

'Well, Frank,' said Charles Forshaw, 'you will concede that I made a good hunchback in — what was it now? It wasn't that thing by Victor Hugo. Anyway, I was the right height for that. *Hopfrog*. That was it. From a story by Edgar Allan Poe.'

There was no reply. Maybe old Frank really *was* asleep.

The third person in the room, a thin, spare man sitting in an upright chair near the fireplace, snapped shut the book that he had been reading and gave a snort of disgust.

'Really, Forshaw,' he said. 'I don't know how you have the patience to put up with that old idiot's insults. Great age doesn't entitle a man to be so damned rude. You shouldn't have brought up that *Macbeth*, though. What about your *Richard the Third*? It was a sensation! People still talk about it. It's a pity you stopped treading the boards and surrendered to the lure of television. You were always a theatre man at heart.'

The thin man patted the pockets of his jacket, trying to locate his pipe and matches. He'd forgotten that the Irving Home no longer permitted smoking anywhere on the premises. He was a fastidious man, who dressed well and cared about his appearance. The few remaining strands of his still dark hair were carefully arranged to cover his balding scalp.

'Anyway,' he said, 'I'm off to bed. Apparently, there's a magician coming tomorrow to entertain us. That was

Gladys's idea. I never had much time for them. Magicians, I mean. We all know it's just a load of legerdemain, so why bother?' He permitted himself a kind of wheezing chuckle. 'Anyway, magicians are for kiddies.'

He hauled himself out of his chair, and walked across the room with the aid of an elegant ebony walking-cane. He turned at the door and said: 'I know you laughed it off, but that barb about your Macbeth must have hurt. Frank Taylor will get himself into trouble one of these days. A sneer too far, you know.'

'Well, Tony, if he wants to get himself into trouble, he'd better hurry up. I don't suppose he'll be around much longer. He's suffering from terminal something-or-other, so Dr Pemberton says.'

'Pemberton's a quack. He said I had a shadow on the lung, but there was nothing there. Pleasant dreams.'

Charles Forshaw watched Anthony Hayling as he walked rather unsteadily out into the corridor and closed the door. He had difficulties with arthritis, but never complained. He was seventy-five, and quite forgotten now, but in 1965 had burst on to the nation's TV screens as Hooper of the Yard. He'd have been — what? — twenty-two. Very handsome, with a shock of black hair, and piercing eyes to match. Millions of people tuned in to Granada TV every Thursday to watch the latest episode of *Hooper*. In 1970 they'd changed the name of the programme to *Crime Scene*, but it was still *Hooper of the Yard* transferred from London to a fictional city in the Home Counties.

There had been no stopping Anthony Hayling. Hollywood had begun to show an interest, even though he had never been in films. Television was his *métier*.

And then, in 1975, it all came to an end. The scandal involving Anthony Hayling had caused such a stir that the then current series of *Crime Scene* had been taken off the air. It didn't do to think of what happened to Hayling in the long years before a few old friends in the Garrick Club — from which he had been expelled — rallied round to get him a place in the Irving Home for Retired Actors.

Forshaw's thoughts were interrupted by Nurse Trickett erupting into the room. She'd come to take old Frank to his quarters, give him his medication, and put him to bed. Gladys Trickett was a single-minded woman, so she simply gave Charles a brief nod before turning her attention to old Frank. With a good deal of fuss, with complaints from the old man and admonitions from the nurse, Frank Taylor was carried off to bed.

Charles Forshaw glanced round the common room. Really, the Irving Home was a very pleasant place in which to live. There was nothing institutionalized about it. Every room in the old mansion was well furnished and cared for. And the company — twelve of them currently in residence — were all interesting men, the majority of them very clubbable.

The Irving Home was an ideal place for people like them to live. Oldminster was large enough to be a real urban hub, a vibrant working town. Its streets were lined with small shops, especially in the old quarter to the west of Cathedral Green. The high street still offered Marks and Spencer, and a busy branch of Next. There was also a Hugo Boss in the town centre, though older men like Forshaw and Hayling preferred to visit a traditional gentlemen's outfitter in Chichester.

The odd thing about the Irving Home, which was opened in 1920, was that it was for male actors only. No women need apply. Perhaps the founder, a rich theatre buff, had thought that a mixed residence would have led to unwelcome vice. The governing committee had held half-hearted discussions about this from time to time, but everyone knew that the Irving Home would remain a single-sex establishment. It followed that to qualify for residency, you had to be either a bachelor, divorced or a widower.

Charles Forshaw glanced at himself in the mirror. He was still a very presentable sort of man, and there was nothing much wrong with him apart from a few common disadvantages consequent on being just over eighty. He had much to be thankful for, particularly a level-headedness that meant he had been content to be a character actor for all of his career. Tony Hayling had exaggerated his success as a leading man, though his Richard the Third had indeed been a triumph. Beneath Hayling's waspish exterior there beat a generous heart.

After his Macbeth had earned him lukewarm reviews, Forshaw had decided that the stage was going to be a dead end for him and, like poor Anthony, he had forged a very successful career in television. He'd enjoyed himself in countless dramas as loyal friends, decent uncles, honest lawyers, Anglican clergymen (he couldn't do RC priests — he didn't sound right, and looked too much like a married man to accept such roles). He'd appeared in a number of dramatizations of Dickens's novels, as various unimportant characters in top hats who hovered on the periphery of the main plot. He'd been Tom Pinch in *Martin Chuzzlewit*, enduring the discomfort of an enormous false bald head. What fun it had all been! People in trains or on buses would often say to him, 'Haven't we met somewhere? I'm sure I've seen you before.' And, of course, they had.

Yes, he'd enjoyed his life as a jobbing actor. But old Frank Taylor . . .

For over thirty years Sir Frank Taylor had dominated the English stage as a sort of second Laurence Olivier. *His* Macbeth had taken London by storm, and had toured with triumphant success through England and Scotland, before embarking on a tour of the American East Coast. In old age, his King Lear, in which he had said a formal goodbye to the stage, had been another triumph. He had done all the major Shakespearean roles, and had also been acclaimed for his interpretation of Ibsen's tortured protagonists. An actor of unique distinction, renowned on stage and screen, he was now, in feeble old age, something of a living legend.

* * *

Later that same night, in a room lit only by the glow of his computer screen, a man who called himself Bosszuallo opened his Tor browser, which would give him unrestricted access to the dark web. He passed from website to website, gleaning information from people whom he trusted, like-minded people with the same goals.

Then, at three o'clock in the morning, he received an email in English from a man who called himself Msciciel. He knew that this man, who lived in Kraków, was a brilliant researcher with committed contacts throughout Europe.

> *Bosszuallo — You are quite right in what you have suggested. You may go ahead now with a clear conscience. You are God's agent in this, and what you will mete out will be His vengeance. — Msciciel.*

Bosszuallo turned off his computer, pushed his chair back, and staggered out of the room. As always, when success was in his grasp, he would be struck down by a migraine — not just a severe headache, but the skull-splitting, debilitating agony that for him would end in sickness and vomiting. What did it mean? Why could he not be left with a clear mind to carry out his mission? He dragged himself to his bed, and succumbed to an uneasy, dream-haunted slumber.

* * *

Not too far away, another dreamer imagined that he was standing once more in the freezing cold of Stutthof, waiting to begin a shuffle through the thick snow. He was only eighteen in the dream but seemed to have aged many years since his carefree childhood in Leipzig. He had known cold winters then, but nothing could compare with the combination of sleet and keen wind in a situation where you were compelled to stand still, doing nothing, while SS-Sturmbannfuhrer Egon Scharnhorst bared his soul to Unterscharfuhrer Schmidt.

'It can't have been anything I said, Unterscharfuhrer,' said Scharnhorst. 'I'm very careful what I say to Helga these days. No, it's something I must have done. So, I thought I'd take her a little present tomorrow. What do you think?'

He removed a glove to delve into one of the pockets of his trench coat. He looked very warm and smart, and a stream of breath hovered above him, made visible in the halo of light from the single bulb above the barrack door.

If we stand here much longer, we'll all drop down dead with cold.

The beautiful emerald necklace sparkled as the major pulled it out of his pocket.

'Oh, she'll like that, sir,' enthused the Unterscharfuhrer. 'She won't be nagging you after she's seen *that*! Did you buy it for her when you went into Danzig last week?'

Major Scharnhorst laughed.

'No, I didn't, you cheeky man! You know very well where I got it. It belonged to a lady who didn't need it anymore, she had an urgent appointment at the crematorium. Anyway, get this lot down to the sheds, and see that they drag all those stinking corpses out into the field at the back of Hut VI. It's too late for them to start digging pits, they can do that tomorrow. We're short-staffed. The Reichsfuhrer would be heartbroken if he could see the state of this place . . .'

At last, the column of living dead began to shuffle through the snow on their way to dispose of the bodies of people who had died in the huts and the infirmary.

He drifted from dream to dream — it was going to be one of those nights, but as hour succeeded hour he knew that he was, in fact, safe and secure in his comfortable bedroom in the Irving Home.

His next dream took him to the British Army Headquarters in the ruins of Hamburg, where he'd been a protégé of Major Mark Rogers, RASC, who had taken a shine to him, and had set him to work first as a procurement assistant, given the task of looting furniture — desks, cupboards, stationery — from two badly bomb-damaged local schools. All these things were needed to furnish Captain Rogers' interrogation centre, part of the denazification programme for the Hamburg-Harburg area. He could hear the good captain's voice now, after a lifetime: 'You speak jolly good English, Shapiro. How do you fancy a spot of interrogation? You could interview some of the lesser fry. We're running short of people to run the city, and these officials can't all have been active Nazis. So, see what you can do.'

Overnight, Germany had become one of the safest places for Jews to live and prosper. With a name like Chaim Jakob Shapiro, he had nothing to fear from the victors. The war was over, and he had survived.

* * *

Gladys Trickett, a state-registered nurse, had been working at the Irving Home for eight years. A no-nonsense woman in her forties, she was immensely proud of her nursing skills, which included putting her elderly charges at ease. She allowed them to tease and joke with her and gave them as good as she got in return. But they knew — all twelve of them — that she wouldn't stand for tantrums, or silly refusals to take their medicine.

The morning after Mervyn Sanders' talk, most of the men were already up — she could hear the whir of electric razors, and the splashing of water in the showers of the en suite bedrooms. Mr Alexander, in room 5, was singing 'Smoke Gets in your Eyes', one of his favourite songs from the fifties. He was eighty-six, and still ramrod straight. She smiled as she passed his door. To look at, he seemed to be a retired senior army officer, a colonel, perhaps, or a brigadier. He'd appeared in countless black-and-white war films in the fifties. Years later, he could still visualize the end credits rolling slowly by. His own name up there on the screen.

Colonel Rycroft . . . Louis Alexander.

General Richardson . . . Louis Alexander.

She entered room 7. Mr Hayling appreciated a little assistance getting dressed as his hands were crippled with arthritis. As she helped him, she glanced at the many framed photographs on the walls. There he was, in all his glory, as

Hooper of the Yard. It was difficult to believe that it was the same man.

'Thank you, Gladys. It'll be breakfast in half an hour. I don't suppose—'

'Yes, Mr Hayling. Cook's doing poached egg and haddock specially for you, as usual.'

'Good, good. You should have married, you know, Gladys. It's no fun for a woman like you looking after us coffin-fodder. Is old Frank up yet?' he went on. 'He was damned rude to Charles Forshaw last night.' And then, changing the subject abruptly again: 'Do you read a lot of German literature?'

'What? No, not as much as I'd like to.' She laughed. 'Don't forget your watch. It's on the bedside table. Why German literature?'

'Well, Goethe — you've heard of Goethe, haven't you? — Goethe said, in one of his little poems, "*Ein alter Mann ist stets ein König Lear*," which means, "An old man is always a King Lear." And that's what Frank Taylor is. He's become the part that he once played. Petulant, childish, stupid and too fond of his own voice. Well, Lear came a cropper, as they say. And Frank will, too, if he doesn't watch out.'

'Can I go, now? Or do you want to indulge in some more character assassination?'

Hayling laughed. He picked up his walking-cane and propelled his spare frame to the door.

'Yes, go, go, by all means. Have you seen my watch?'

Gladys Trickett left the room. Time to help Sir Frank Taylor, their resident King Lear, to face a new day. He could neither lie down nor get up without assistance, and when helping the frailer residents, she always left him to the last, to give him that extra little lie-in. She opened the door of room 2, and went in. She crossed to the window, and pulled back the curtains. Then she turned to the bed.

Gladys was not a screamer, but she almost fainted with shock. Sir Frank Taylor lay still on his back, the sheet drawn up under his chin, his eyes closed. Ninety-four years old, he had died in his bed; but it was not old age that had ended his life. The bedclothes were saturated in blood, and an ebony-handled dagger had been driven through his heart.

This couldn't be real. It was an illusion. She closed her eyes, desperate to shut out the scene before her. But when she opened them again, it was all still *there*. Red stains, pale sheets. She uttered a shriek of anguish and ran to the door — so fast she almost collided with one of the men going down to the dining room. He glanced at the bed, pale and trembling, and she heard him whisper: 'So much blood. *So much blood . . .*'

* * *

'What have you got for me?'

Detective Inspector Paul French winced at the banality of his own routine question. He didn't really need Dr Raymond Dunwoody, the medical examiner, to tell him that this was murder, an attack on a frail old man, who still lay on his back in the blood-sodden bed.

Ray Dunwoody had finished his preliminary examination of the body, and sat on a chair near the window, while the scene-of-crime officers moved about their essential tasks. He leaned forward, his shoulders hunched as though he was already exhausted by his grim work.

'What have I got for you? I've got a man of ninety-four, stabbed through the heart. The nurse tells me that he was suffering from a medical condition that would have proved fatal in just a few months. I haven't seen his own doctor, yet.'

'No sign of a struggle?'

'No. There are no defensive wounds to the hands or arms. He was wearing his pyjamas, and the bedclothes were pulled up to his chin. His eyes were closed. I think he died instantly without waking or knowing that he had been attacked. I'd say he's been dead for five hours. Four or five hours. I'll know more once I've done an autopsy.'

DI French looked down at the famous actor. Frail and shrivelled, Frank Taylor looked as though he had just been unearthed from an Egyptian tomb.

'Where's the crime-scene manager?'

'He's in the next room — it's vacant at the moment. Alan Wickes from Rose Hill nick. Do you know him? He seems a thorough kind of chap, very keen on protocol. A bit stand-offish, but a good bloke, as far as I can see.'

'I'm told there was a dagger—'

'Yes, it's over there, in one of those plastic boxes. It really *is* a dagger, part of the ceremonial uniform of an SS officer, I'd guess. There's no mistaking the insignia stamped on the thing . . . Wickes reckons it's a replica, the kind of thing you can buy over the internet.'

'An SS dagger?' French was taken aback. 'That's not a normal spur-of-the-moment weapon. What did Sir Frank Taylor have to do with the SS?'

Ray shrugged. 'I don't know, Paul, that's not my line of business. There may be all kinds of mementoes lying around in a place like this. Maybe this dagger was something like that. Something lying conveniently to hand, you know.'

'Maybe. You know,' French smiled wryly, 'for someone who claims that detection isn't his line of business, you're doing a great job.'

Dunwoody chuckled darkly. 'There is something else, though, a possible connection between Sir Frank Taylor and the Nazis. Look at this.' He stood up and drew back the bed sheet from the dead man's right arm. The shrivelled skin was disfigured by a long scar.

'This looks like a long-healed scar — possibly from an acid burn,' he said. 'Some people did that to remove their concentration camp number, I've read. Given his age, Sir Frank could have been an inmate of a Nazi concentration camp.'

'An inmate?' said French. 'Was he Jewish?'

'Well, I don't know — he could have been. There are all kinds of myths about his origins. His fans all love that side of him . . . the mystery. He was supposed to be the illegitimate son of a Russian princess, though others said that he was descended from Polish nobility — and there were a lot of Poles killed in Auschwitz. Nobody knew for certain, though I expect you'll dig up all kinds of documents while you investigate this crime.'

'So—'

'So, I must get this body to the morgue. I need to do a full autopsy, and I want Sir Frank's own doctor to be present when I do so.' Ray gave French a worried look. 'I'll leave the detecting to you.'

* * *

'I don't know,' said Wickes. 'Maybe we're looking at a hate crime of some sort. Anti-Semitism rearing its ugly head?'

The scene-of-crime manager and DI French were sitting at a table in room 1 of the Irving Home, next to Sir Frank's room. Each was slightly wary of the other. Alan Wickes was a giant of a man, with broad shoulders; he seemed to be bursting out of his CSI suit. He had a heavy, frog-like face, and slightly protuberant eyes. DI French knew this type of officer. He would be a stolid, unimaginative man, with a close eye for detail and the possessor of an innate efficiency. There was not much that he would miss.

Wickes in turn looked at French. He looked like the typical office-bound bobby who'd long forgotten what it was like to be out on the beat or touring the sleazier areas of the town at night in a fuggy squad car. His hair was thinning, and he wore old-fashioned rimless glasses. Still, DI Wickes knew it had been him and his sergeant who'd solved the murder at Renfield Hall last year, and most people in the force agreed that he was a good detective.

'Can you tell me about this dagger?' asked French. 'Dr Dunwoody says you thought it was a replica of some sort.'

'Yes, that's what I think. There's a lot of that type of thing about. Memorabilia. Most of it's fake. We've emptied the contents of Sir Frank Taylor's bureau, and boxed it all up for you. There's quite a lot of stuff — letters, certificates, theatre programmes, all sorts of stuff.' He suddenly smiled, and the smile transformed his austere, heavy features. 'Before you got here, sir, an old guy rushed into the room before we could stop him, and shouted: "Are all thy conquests, something-or-others, triumphs, spoils, shrunk to this little measure? Fare thee well!" It was so realistic that I just stood there, gawping at him. Then he rushed out again.'

'Isn't that a quote from *Julius Caesar*?'

'Yes, it was. And earlier, another old bloke tried out a bit of *Macbeth*.' He chuckled wryly and shook his head. 'Well, we're finished here. We'll send everything over to you at Jubilee House later this morning.'

'Thanks. I'll cast my own eye over the crime scene, and when my sergeant gets here, I'll interview the staff and residents. Somebody may have seen or heard something. And then we'll take it from there.'

The burly man rose to his feet. His head almost touched the ceiling.

'Can I give you a word of advice, Inspector French?' he said. 'While you're listening to their stories, don't forget that *they're all actors*. They could lie their heads off and seem to be telling God's honest truth.'

4. THE VIEW FROM BELOW-STAIRS

DI French stood at a window in the wide vestibule of the Irving Home, watching Wickes supervising his team as they loaded all their spoil into a police van. It was only when they had disappeared down the winding drive that the massive crime-scene manager carefully inserted himself into his black Skoda Fabia and followed them.

DI French gave an involuntary sigh of relief. He found it difficult to concentrate on a case while the SOCOs were present. They flitted about like nuns, talking quietly to each other only when it was necessary to do so. Like Trappists. Were there such things as Trappist nuns?

It had suddenly become quiet in the vestibule: the residents were either in their rooms or being supervised discreetly but no doubt firmly elsewhere. Once over her initial shock, Nurse Trickett had quickly assumed command of her thespian troupe.

All that French could hear now was the sonorous ticking of a grandfather clock. He glanced around him, and silently approved of the clock, the oak chest facing the front entrance, and the well-polished oval table, on which an array of magazines was displayed. There was *Country Life* which Moira liked to read, and *The Field*, jostling for position with

Oldshire Life, the rather pretentious county magazine. The place smelled of lavender furniture polish and old woodwork.

He reached into his pocket, and brought out his new iPhone, a birthday present from Moira, and called Sergeant Glyn Edwards. It was time for his right-hand man to join him at the Irving Home for Retired Actors. Half an hour later, DS Edwards arrived at the home, slightly out of breath. 'Good morning, sir,' he said politely, before stammering, 'though it's not really, is it? Who could possibly want to murder Sir Frank Taylor? He was ninety-four, for God's sake.'

French looked at his sergeant. He'd obviously dressed very quickly, as his tie was protruding from under his collar. He'd told him not to bother with a tie, as long as he wore a proper shirt, but Glyn was evidently a stickler for etiquette. He was wearing a decent leather jacket and black trousers, and he still favoured leather lace-up shoes over more comfortable footwear. He was thirty-eight, but beginning to look older.

'Well, it's our job,' he said, 'to find out who murdered Sir Frank Taylor, so your question was, I assume, rhetorical. Now, I'll tell you what we're going to do — have you had any breakfast this morning?'

'Well, there wasn't much time, sir. I had a piece of toast.'

'Yes, I can see the crumbs around your mouth.' He smiled slightly as Edwards hurriedly wiped his face. 'The ambulance will be here soon, to take Sir Frank's body away, so you'd better come with me. I want you to see the body before we get down to business. After that, we'll go and interview Nurse Trickett, and then whoever we find in the kitchen.'

'Why the kitchen, sir?'

'Because while we're there, you can ask them for something to eat.'

They lifted the blue and white police tape and entered the room. Sir Frank Taylor still lay as French had last seen him, stained bedclothes drawn up close beneath his chin, and French had the sudden feeling that this room would retain the awful taint of death for months to come.

'Sir Frank was stabbed through the heart. A single blow would have killed him.' He snorted suddenly. 'Everything I say this morning sounds like a quote from Shakespeare. It's all these actors, Glyn. We've already had two of them spouting the Bard. Now I'm doing it!'

'Perhaps they've decided to stage a do-it-yourself *Macbeth*, with poor Sir Frank as King Duncan. It's supposed to bring bad luck to mention *Macbeth* in theatrical circles. They have to call it "The Scottish Play".'

'Well, if that was the case, there was a glaring anachronism in their performance. Sir Frank was killed with a Nazi ceremonial dagger. And Dunwoody told me—'

'A *Nazi* dagger? I don't like the sound of that, sir. It's the 21 April today.'

'You're losing me, Sergeant. What are you trying to tell me?'

'Well, sir, I'd never have known. But it came up in the pub quiz and the date sort of stuck in my head . . . yesterday was the anniversary of Hitler's birthday.'

* * *

Gladys Trickett sat behind her tidy desk and gave all her attention to the two detectives. She approved of French. She admired his blue pin-striped suit, which had a hint of white handkerchief at the breast pocket. He wore elegant rimless glasses, though she noticed that they were covered in milky fingerprints, and when he had reached into his pocket for a notebook, he had brought out a dummy with it. Although long past the first flush of youth, he evidently had a baby at home.

The gloomy sergeant on the other hand looked slightly more scruffy and tired. Were those crumbs on his jacket?

'Nurse Trickett?' DI French interrupted her train of thought. 'I just asked you about the security of the home and grounds?'

'Security, Inspector? Of course, let me explain. This house was built in 1867 and back then it had four entrances,

32

one at the front, one on the south side, and two at the back, facing the ornamental gardens. When the house was adapted as a residential home in the 1920s, two of the entrances were bricked up, so now there is only the front door, and one rear door at the end of what we call the garden passage.'

'Presumably these doors are locked at night?'

'Yes, they're both locked at ten o'clock, once all the residents are accounted for. One or two of the more able-bodied residents go down to the Coach and Horses in the village. If they get back late, there's a bell they can ring. But that kind of thing's very rare. And yes, before you ask, both doors are covered by CCTV. But I've already looked and once the doors were locked nobody went in or out — the doors remained closed all night. I'm afraid we're still analogue here so I can't email you the footage, but I've given the tapes to your crime-scene manager.'

'What about the rooms?' asked DS Edwards. 'Are they locked at night, as well?'

Nurse Trickett laughed.

'*Locked*? This isn't a lunatic asylum, Sergeant, though at times . . .' She tried to look serious, but laughed again. 'Oh, I know this is no joking matter, but they're a lively bunch, are my actors, and at times it can be bedlam here when they mull over their earlier careers. They act things out, so that the common room resembles a repertory company, like those nice people at the Playhouse in Oldminster town centre. No, the rooms aren't locked, but they can be bolted from the inside.'

'What if someone were to be taken ill in the night? After all, they're all a bit old, aren't they?'

'We can open the doors from the outside, with a kind of screwdriver. They're the kind of locks that you find on toilet cubicles in hospitals.'

'Hm . . . Well, Nurse Trickett,' said French, 'thank you for your time. It's early days yet, but I must warn you that this could have been an inside job. We'll need to interview all the residents, and also the domestic staff. Can you give me a list—' Before he could finish, she had handed him a typed list of staff.

'There are fourteen of us at the moment,' she said. 'Four of us are state-registered nurses: myself, Jean Buckley, Mary Helm and Gabriel Swift. There's Tracey Potter, a general dogsbody, who works mornings. George Cavanagh is the resident house manager, and our handyman, Gareth Pugh, lives out. Terry Lucas is the gardener. He lives by himself in the lodge by the main gate. Then there's Trudy Vosper, the receptionist, and the PA, Cathy Billington, who works for both me and George Cavanagh. Oh, then there's the cook, Teddy Balonek. He lives in a flat on the second floor. That's just a list of names, I know, Inspector, but they'll turn into real people once you've interviewed them.'

Yes, just a list of names, thought French, though one of them, Tracey Potter, rang a faint bell.

'Where's Mr Cavanagh this morning?'

'He's in town. He went there last night on business with the trustees, and was due to attend a meeting this morning with Bishop Poindexter, the chairman. He's staying at the palace for the night. Do you want me to get him back?'

'No, that won't be necessary, but I'll want to see him when he returns. We'd like to talk to some of the domestic staff today. We'll interview the residents tomorrow, when, hopefully, they will have recovered from the shock. You've been of enormous help to us, Miss Trickett.'

* * *

Glyn sat with French at the scrubbed kitchen table, devouring a bacon sandwich washed down with a mug of tea. He'd already noted that the kitchen was a full industrial model, and that the cook, a man of thirty or so, who had introduced himself as Teddy Balonek, was clearly a trained professional. Three members of the domestic staff had joined them for breakfast; at the far end of the room a teenage girl was loading plates and cups into a dishwasher.

'We all liked him,' said Teddy. 'He was a lovely old man. He'd come in here some days for a glass of warm milk, and he'd tell us some of his adventures when he was a young man. He was a "sir", but there was no side on him. He'd been with us for nearly ten years. It's not right. He was in the war. All kinds of adventures he'd had.'

'This bacon sandwich is first class.' Glyn set it down reluctantly and pulled out his notebook, aware that he was supposed to be working. 'Do you mind my asking you to spell your surname? It's not one I've heard before. Croatian, is it?'

Teddy looked a bit annoyed at the question, and Glyn wondered if he'd touched a nerve, but when the cook spoke he sounded unconcerned. 'It's Polish. B-A-L-O-N-E-K. My grandfather was in the Polish Free Forces, then he came back after the war when things got a bit difficult in the late 1970s, along with my parents. Probably why I liked listening to Frank's stories so much.' He saw Glyn's interest had drifted back to the sandwich. 'That's Wiltshire bacon I grilled for you, Sergeant. We get it sent up specially from Hanbury's in town.'

One of the other members of staff, a thin woman in a drab skirt and dull orange top, added her bit of information.

'I'm not surprised Sir Frank's been murdered,' she said. 'They've been after him for years. It must have been the Nazis, or maybe the Communists, but they got him in the end.'

DI French looked at the woman. Was he to be told something of relevance, or was she just fantasizing? So many people did that when they wanted to appear important to the police.

'What do you mean by that, madam? You know for certain that his life was in danger? I didn't catch your name.'

'That's because I never told you it. "Madam" indeed! I'm Liz Bold, the daily cleaner. Now, I haven't got any qualifications, Inspector, but I'm no fool, and what I heard I heard.'

A weather-beaten man in brown overalls laughed.

'I'm Gareth Pugh,' he said. 'I'm the general handyman. Half the things she tells us she makes up, don't you, Liz? But — well, you did tell us about that man who threatened him, and now he's dead, so . . .'

'Ms Bold,' said French, contriving to give an edge to his voice, 'will you please tell me about this man. Who was he? And when did he threaten Sir Frank Taylor?'

Liz Bold patted her hair and sat up straight. It wasn't often that she was the centre of attention.

'It was over five years ago, now,' she began, 'in 2013. I always try to hoover the gentlemen's rooms while they're at breakfast. Well, it was early October — I remember that, on account of my Winona getting engaged to that Billy Loach. I warned her, but you know what girls are. And you see how *that* turned out!'

'She was well rid of him, Liz,' said Teddy. 'That boy she's living with now is a much nicer lad.'

French cleared his throat. 'Could we perhaps get back to the matter in hand? Did someone threaten Sir Frank or not? What's this Billy Loach got to do with it?'

'Oh, *he's* nothing to do with it,' said Liz. 'So, I was in room 3, and had just finished the dusting, when I heard voices coming from next door — Sir Frank's room. Even in those days Nurse Trickett would leave old Sir Frank to the last, so he was still there, in his room. I couldn't hear what he was saying, because his voice seemed to have gone all tiny and wobbly, but I heard another voice clearly say, "You're as rich as Croesus and there's those in Birmingham who are still waiting for their money. We've ways of making you cough up, Chaim, so gather your wits and pay your debts now, or it'll be the worse for you." That's what this man said.'

'He called Sir Frank *Chaim*? You're sure it wasn't "chum"?'

'No, it was Chaim. Maybe it was a nickname. I don't know.'

Liz evidently has a reputation for making things up, DI French thought, but this story seemed to be a recollection of something that had really happened. *Chaim* . . .

'Did you see this man? The man talking to Sir Frank?' asked French.

'No. I had to continue cleaning the room next door, but I asked Sir Frank later whether everything was all right, and he got quite shirty — "why shouldn't everything be all right", and so on. I said nothing after that, except to the staff.'

'I think I saw the guy, though,' Gareth Pugh put in. 'I was cleaning the windows when I saw this man hurrying round the side of the house from the back entrance. He was a big, burly man, with a shock of white hair. He was what I'd call light on his feet. He drove off in a green Ford Fiesta.'

'And this was five years ago? Did the man ever come back?'

'No. Not as far as we know,' said Gareth.

A smattering of facts. They may well lead somewhere. Gareth Pugh was evidently a keen observer of men. Maybe there were other things he'd seen and stored away. French pushed back his chair and stood up.

'Well, thank you very much for feeding my sergeant,' he said. 'It's been very interesting talking to you. Tomorrow it'll be the residents' turn.'

Liz Bold laughed. 'It's them that'll be talking to *you*,' she said. 'You won't be able to get a word in edgeways. You're a new audience.'

As Glyn made to follow French out of the kitchen, the girl at the dishwasher shyly pulled him by the sleeve.

'You don't remember me, do you?' she asked. He looked at her and instantly unlocked that part of his memory where she had been stored more than a year earlier.

'Of course I remember you,' he said. 'You're Tracey Potter, and you were such a help to me over that business at Renfield Hall. How are you? And how's your friend Shona? Does she still paint all her fingernails different colours?'

Tracey giggled, but made no reply. Instead, still clutching his sleeve, she pulled him out into the corridor. Her voice dropped to a whisper.

'Listen, Sergeant,' she said. 'Poor Sir Frank was stabbed to death with a German dagger, wasn't he? My dad will murder *me* when he finds out we've had a murder here. So will Mum. She's had to have two teeth out, so she's been real mean to me all week.'

Glyn recalled his first meeting with Tracey and her friend Shona. They had come to volunteer information that had proved to be of considerable value in the Renfield case, and had sat, pale and frightened, on the opposite side of his desk. He'd sworn them both to secrecy, and had sent them down to the staff canteen for a free sandwich each. He'd liked the vulnerable girl then and warmed to her now. She had a kindly innocence about her that he found appealing.

'It's supposed to be a secret, Tracey,' he said, 'but yes, he was stabbed to death with a Nazi dagger.'

'The Nazis fought us in the war,' said Tracey. 'They were Germans, but they had to be called Nazis cos Mr Churchill said so. Hitler was their leader, and he died in a bunk.'

'Right . . .' Tracey's history was a little . . . off, but he thought he'd press his advantage and see if she knew anything more. 'And this dagger—'

'I know whose it was. It wasn't Sir Frank's. It belonged to Mr Hayling.'

'Mr Hayling had a Nazi dagger?'

'Yes. I saw it once, on top of that little bookcase under his window. It had a swastika on it. A swastika was a kind of cross, only on one side, with little ends. It meant that you were a Nazi if you sewed it on to your coat.'

'Yes, I know what a swastika is, thanks Tracey. Once again, you've helped the police, and you can tell your dad that. And your mum, too.'

So, the dagger had belonged to Anthony Hayling. Another fact. Another interesting starting point for their investigation into the murder of Sir Frank Taylor.

He went to find DI French who listened carefully to this new information before nodding his approval.

'I'm going to leave the residents to stew in their own juice for the rest of the day, Glyn,' said DI French. 'They need to recover from the shock of this murder before we question them. They're all old, and some of them are frail. And in any case, an interval for retrospection might sharpen their wits. But we'll make sure to question Mr Hayling first.'

* * *

As it was growing dusk Anthony Hayling left the house through the rear door and made his way slowly along the edge of the lawn to the vegetable garden. As he had expected, Terry Lucas was there.

'Good evening, Terry,' he said. 'You don't mind if I have a smoke, do you? It's strictly forbidden in the house, but I know you won't tell on me.'

'Of course I won't, Mr Hayling, sir,' said Terry. 'In fact, I think I'll join you. That's what they call aiding and abetting, but I know you'd never grass on me either.'

They both sat down on a garden bench. Terry lit a cigarette. Hayling produced his pipe and tobacco. There was a flurry of matches, and then the two men sat in silence for a while, watching the sun go down beyond the trees.

'This is a bad business about Sir Frank,' said Hayling at length. 'Bad for its own sake, of course, but also bad for the likes of you and me.'

Terry glanced at his companion, but said nothing. He knew what Hayling meant.

'We'll need to keep our heads down, Terry, until the police have gone, though I expect they'll be nosing around here for days.'

Terry stood up, threw down his cigarette butt, and ground it into the grass with his heel.

'Don't worry, sir,' he said. 'What happened to Sir Frank had nothing to do with you or me. We both know that. If they ask you anything, just give them straight answers. You saw nothing. You heard nothing. Come on, let me give you a hand up.'

He gently helped Anthony Hayling to his feet, gave him his walking-cane, and watched him as he walked slowly and painfully back to the house.

Poor old sod, he thought, *he's the best of the lot*. But then, he and Mr Hayling had both done time, a shattering experience that could have done for a lesser man.

* * *

Ray Dunwoody stood beside the now sewn-up corpse of Sir Frank Taylor, which lay in one of the dissecting rooms at the police mortuary. Beside him was Dr Rollo Pemberton, a drooping kind of man of sixty or so, who was the official physician to the Irving Home for Retired Actors. Both men had removed their green surgical gowns and masks, and were about to discard their latex gloves.

'It was very civil of you to let me assist you today, Dunwoody,' said Dr Pemberton. 'You could clearly see the extent of the cancer. He wouldn't have lasted more than a few weeks, poor old fellow. But all his other organs were in remarkably good shape, apart from his left lung, which showed the beginnings of tubercular lesion. He'd broken two ribs at some time in the past, but they'd healed well. And his heart was remarkably sound — at least, until someone destroyed it with a dagger.'

'One single blow killed him instantly. Do you think the killer may have had some medical knowledge?'

'Possibly. As we both saw, the blade penetrated just below the left atrium and into the left ventricle. Death would have been instantaneous. The killer may have had medical knowledge, but it could have been sheer luck that he didn't make a mess.'

'What's the general state of health among your old actors, Doctor?' Dunwoody asked. 'Are they generally mobile?'

Rollo Pemberton gave his colleague a shrewd glance.

'"Mobile", eh? Mobile enough to slip into a fellow thespian's room in the night and murder him? I can't see it, myself. One of them suffers hideously from arthritis — that's Mr Hayling, a famous actor in his day. Others have slight difficulties walking. Otherwise they're in quite good shape. A couple of dicky hearts. Shadows on the lung. Angina. That kind of thing. Quite frankly, I can't see any of them as potential murderers. We'll just have to wait and see what Paul French and that sergeant of his come up with.'

5. THE CAST WAS AS FOLLOWS

'Terrible! *Terrible!* I'll tell you at once, officers, no one here at the Irving Home could have done this. We all loved old Frank. He was part of the fabric of England, a name to rank with that group of giants that includes Dirk Bogarde, Sean Connery and Michael Caine. All England mourns.'

DI French silently demurred. It was quite possible that somebody at the Irving Home had killed Sir Frank Taylor, but this attractive elderly man, Charles Forshaw, had to be allowed his illusions. French did not doubt the actor's sincerity, but had noted with a certain wry amusement that he couldn't resist a few theatrical flourishes. Part of the fabric of England? Well, maybe.

The sitting room of Charles Forshaw's suite was crammed with battered but genuine antique furniture, and memorabilia. A Boulle cabinet, its doors gaping open, held a collection of what were evidently scrapbooks. Framed theatrical posters covered the walls. A bookcase bulged with books on stage history, and paperback copies of plays. He and Forshaw were sitting in comfortable armchairs on either side of a fireplace containing a double-bar electric fire, while DS Edwards perched on an upright chair near the door.

'And you heard and saw nothing, Mr Forshaw?' asked Glyn. 'No unusual noise in the night — doors opening — things like that?'

'I heard nothing, Sergeant. I'm a heavy sleeper. I still can't believe it. *Stabbed*? Frank was repeatedly stabbed in three separate productions of *Julius Caesar* — you may have seen the famous one at the Haymarket, with the young Richard Burton as Brutus — but he was never stabbed in real life. Not till now. What I'm trying to say is, it would have been much easier to smother old Frank with a pillow. He was very frail, you know. Using a dagger must have *meant* something.'

Yes, thought French, Forshaw was right about that. The Nazi dagger must have had some significance. Whatever it was, he and Glyn Edwards would root it out.

'You know, Mr Forshaw,' he said, 'I'm sure I've seen you before. It was a good while ago. You and another gentleman were collecting for a charity, and you were having some kind of altercation . . . I'm sure it was you.'

Charles Forshaw roared with laughter.

'It *was* me. You saw me as one of the two good men rebuffed by Ebenezer Scrooge in Granada's TV production of *A Christmas Carol* in 1982, I think it was. People often think they've met character actors like me in real life.'

'Why, yes — of course! You were very convincing, too. You seem very active, Mr Forshaw.'

'I know what you're going to say, Inspector. Why don't I do some television again? Well, I'd jump at the chance of a few cameo roles, but the truth is, I can't remember lines as I could when I was still working. No, I'm very happy as I am.'

'I admire you for that, Mr Forshaw. When did you last see Sir Frank Taylor?'

'Two nights ago, about eleven o'clock. We'd had a guest speaker in — Mervyn Sanders, the antiques man — and when he'd gone, we started to reminisce about roles we'd undertaken in the old days.'

'One moment, Mr Forshaw,' Edwards said, scribbling in his notebook. 'What time did Mr Sanders leave?'

'About ten, it was. Now, you *can't* suspect Mr Sanders, detective — he's a sweet fellow, nervous type. His family were killed by the Nazis, you know. Anyway, I showed him to the door myself and heard it click shut behind him.'

'Yes, sir. And what happened after that?'

'Then Nurse Trickett came to carry old Frank off to bed. And that was the last time I saw him.'

He angrily brushed away a single tear that had rolled down his cheek.

'Sorry about that, gentlemen. We're supposed to be an emotional lot — "luvvies", they call us, don't they? A silly, brainless word. But when you've passed eighty, you're permitted the occasional tear.'

'Was Sir Frank Taylor ever addressed as Chaim?'

'*What?* What do you mean by that?' Forshaw's handsome face flushed red with sudden anger. 'What are you suggesting? His friends called him Frank. Other people used his title.' He made to stand up. 'You'll have to excuse me now. I always need a little nap mid-morning.'

Charles Forshaw's eyes settled on a framed black-and-white photograph on the mantelpiece. It was of a beautiful woman wearing an elegant evening gown. She was looking upwards towards the left into a haze of nebulous light. Glyn Edwards followed his gaze, and gave a slight exclamation.

'Is that a picture of Coretta Grierson, who starred with James Mason in *Death by Candlelight*?' he exclaimed. 'Did you act with her, sir?'

Forshaw chuckled. He seemed to have recovered his good humour and sat back down in front of the electric fire. Evidently, he was ready to postpone his nap for a moment longer.

'Quite the film buff, aren't you, Sergeant? Coretta Grierson was my wife, but we never appeared in anything together.' He gave a twinkling smile, obviously reminiscing about his beautiful partner. 'Well, I think that's all I can tell you, gentlemen. But if you want to ask me any further questions at a later date, you'll always find me here.'

He glanced at the photograph of Coretta Grierson again; they saw the tears welling up in his eyes.

'Well, Glyn,' said DI French as they stood in the corridor outside Charles Forshaw's room, 'I hit a nerve there. So, according to Liz and Gareth Pugh, a well-built, white-haired man who was light on his feet came all the way from Birmingham to see Sir Frank, to threaten him, and this man addressed him as Chaim, which is a popular Jewish name.'

'So you think Frank Taylor was Jewish?'

'Ray Dunwoody told me that Sir Frank had been ritually circumcised, and that something, presumably a tattoo, had been removed from his forearm. From which we may conclude that Sir Frank Taylor was Jewish — and very possibly a Holocaust survivor — who was murdered with a Nazi dagger. But why did Forshaw react the way he did at the mention of "Chaim"?'

* * *

'It's most unfortunate,' said Anthony Hayling. 'We're like a gentlemen's club here, Inspector, not accustomed to being exposed to public scrutiny. Now, I've no doubt, hordes of reporters will descend on us, and we won't be able to walk in the grounds.'

'Yes . . . I'm sure you're very sad that Sir Frank Taylor should have met such a terrible end,' said French in an attempt to draw Hayling away from the subject of himself.

'I suffer badly from arthritis,' said the old actor. 'I need a decent daily walk in our private gardens here if I'm to avoid being confined to a wheelchair. I'm not terribly old — but old enough . . . I used to take a walk down Upper Temple Street, admiring the cherry trees in spring, but had to stop after an unfortunate encounter.'

'What kind of encounter, Mr Hayling?'

'It was a lady. She looked at me, and her face lit up. "Oh!" she cried. "You're Hooper of the Yard!" And then I saw the smile flee from her face as she recalled — well, never mind all that. I paid dearly for my indiscretions.'

Anthony Hayling, like many actors of his generation, had achieved success partly through his good looks, and his distinctive voice. Mumbling was unknown (and anathema) to people like him, and Charles Forshaw. He was well dressed, in a brown double-breasted suit with a smart white shirt and some sort of club tie. A red silk handkerchief adorned his top pocket. *If I don't jolly him out of his self-preoccupation,* French thought, *we'll be here all day.*

'You didn't like Sir Frank Taylor, did you, Mr Hayling?' French was taking a risk here, but he decided to trust his instincts.

'No, since you ask me so bluntly, I didn't like him.' Hayling snorted. 'In fact, I detested him. He was a rude, domineering has-been, who claimed a sort of pre-eminence here to which he wasn't entitled. He was never in the same league as Richard Burton, and his claim to be the equal of James Mason was simply laughable. You should have heard him the other night, belittling Charles Forshaw's early stage work: there was jealousy in every envenomed syllable.'

The actor was getting into his stride. He seemed to be enjoying himself, and each word he uttered revealed his own deep-seated jealousy of the famous Sir Frank Taylor. But just when French was about to curb the tide of the actor's obvious hatred, Hayling suddenly asked an apparently irrelevant question.

'Do you speak German, Inspector?'

'No, sir, I don't—'

'He could never quite rid himself of his German accent. Frank, I mean. You can hear it in those old films he made: particularly his s's and t's. Frank Taylor wasn't all that he cracked himself up to be. If I were you, I'd look into his past for someone out for revenge. And look outside the home, nobody here at the Irving Home is capable of killing anyone — except on the stage, of course.'

'Are you saying that Sir Frank Taylor was German?'

'No. I'm saying that he had traces of a German accent. That's not the same thing.'

Where is all this leading? French thought, feeling a little bewildered. *Time to attack.*

'Do you own a Nazi-era dagger? It was with such a weapon that Sir Frank Taylor was killed, and someone saw a dagger here, in your room, on top of that bookcase in the window.'

The actor blushed with evident vexation.

'Nonsense! Whoever it was must have been mistaken. Why on earth would I have a Nazi dagger? I'm not interested in things like that, but Frank was. Now I come to think of it, *he* had a dagger. You look through his things. He has books of black-and-white photographs from before and during the war — family snaps, yes, but also pictures of the Nazi bigwigs. Frank was an enigma, if ever there was one.'

Glyn had so far said nothing. He had been gazing fascinated at the retired actor, a man with sparse hair, a man crippled with arthritis. For the last three weeks he had been watching re-runs of *Hooper of the Yard* on the Talking Pictures TV channel. He had followed the adventures of the handsome, dashing Scotland Yard superintendent with the shock of black hair as he and his colleagues bundled themselves into a sedate Wolseley saloon car and dashed off to the scene of a crime, the little silver bell fixed above the front bumper heralding their approach. His powerful, urgent voice had dominated every scene, ably supported by his faithful sergeant, Johnny Pepper. And here he was now, a shadow of that man, but the same man nonetheless, though the voice was higher pitched, and petulant. It was Glyn's turn to ask a question.

'Mr Hayling,' he said, 'did you ever hear anybody address Sir Frank Taylor as Chaim?'

'No. I don't think he wanted to be reminded of his earlier days. He was always Frank to everybody in the acting profession.'

'We heard that he once had a visitor who addressed him as Chaim. Somebody from Birmingham.'

'Well, maybe so. As you probably know, his real name was Chaim Jakob Shapiro.' When he registered the shock on their faces, he looked triumphant. 'Ah!' he cried. 'So you *didn't* know that! Well, he didn't talk about his past in interviews — it's certainly not something you'll find in a film book or on the internet. He wanted to forget the whole business. He was a German Jew, who somehow escaped from one of those concentration camps. He told me that, years ago. Obviously, I never mentioned it to anyone else . . . the old fellow himself seemed to have buried all that. And it didn't stop him being an arrogant bully.'

* * *

'I can't make that man out,' said French as they left the old actor's room. 'He wants us to believe that Sir Frank was obsessed with the war and the Nazis, and then talks about him being Jewish. There's something ironic about that. Let's go and hear what our other retired thespians have to say.'

None of the other residents of the Irving Home for Retired Actors had seen or heard anything unusual during the night of the murder either. But a number of them had something to add to the picture of Sir Frank Taylor, alias Chaim Jakob Shapiro. Louis Alexander, a retired film actor, admitted that, like Hayling, he had found Sir Frank Taylor something of an enigma.

'You'll hear all kinds of rumours about where he came from, Inspector. All nonsense, I expect. And I wouldn't give too much credence to that Jewish ancestry. He used to hint at it, you know, but I think that if you really delved deep enough, you'd find that he was the son of a school teacher in Balham or a mill-worker in Bradford . . . something like that.

'Did you know that I was with him in *Only the Brave*? I played Major Porter, the general's adjutant. He and I used to consume boxes of Capstan Full Strength between takes. I always got on well with him, and I'm very angry that he's been murdered. Terrible. Terrible.'

'What do you think of Mr Anthony Hayling?' asked DS Edwards.

'Hayling? A man much wronged. Kind and generous. He'd give you his last penny if you were in trouble. Yes, much wronged. Hayling is in constant pain, but never complains.'

Donald Mordaunt, a retired repertory actor, had known Sir Frank Taylor for over thirty years.

'Even at the height of his powers he could find time to advise my kind of actor, the ones who know they'll never move beyond a few provincial theatres. Even when his *Lear* had taken London by storm, he found time to come down to Richmond where I was appearing as Inspector Goole in *An Inspector Calls*. I couldn't get it right — there was no force, no conviction in my performance. He sat through Act I, and then asked the director whether he could take charge for a few minutes. "Your blocking's all wrong," he said, and there and then he got down on his knees and drew fresh lines on the stage with a piece of chalk. Then we started the act again, both he and I reading the part aloud and in unison. Gradually, he took over, and my voice faded away, then suddenly he stopped, and I found myself continuing with his voice and his mannerisms. Well, I received three curtain calls after the first performance, and that was Frank's doing. I'll never forget him, and will always honour his memory.'

The only other resident who had anything to offer was a cheerful Cockney man in jeans and T-shirt. DS Edwards recognized him immediately. His name was Sam Gossage, but Glyn knew him as Johnny Pepper, Anthony Hayling's faithful sergeant in *Hooper of the Yard*.

'So, you recognize me, do you, my man?' said Gossage. He gave a good-humoured laugh. 'It was fun working with Tony Hayling. I had my cameo roles, forever being coshed on the head, tied up, thrown in the Thames — marvellous, it was. And then Tony went and blotted his copybook, and that was that. But I was never out of work. I specialized in "salt of the earth" roles — reformed burglars, costermongers, all sorts. I once appeared opposite Jack Hawkins as a murderous private soldier who'd barricaded himself into a derelict building. Jack was the typical officer in his British warm and bowler hat. "Give yourself up, Tommy," he pleaded, and I did! Great fun, all of it.'

'What was your opinion of Sir Frank Taylor?' asked DI French.

'Well, gents,' said Gossage, 'Anthony Hayling was a brilliant actor. We just pass the time of day now, because he was always a gentleman, and I'm not. I really am a Cockney, you know, born within the sound of Bow Bells. But we were a triumph together in *Hooper of the Yard*.'

'And what did you think of Sir Frank Taylor?' French persisted.

Gossage sighed. 'Sir Frank Taylor was a mean and devious caricature of what a great actor should be. He was like something from a Victorian melodrama, overblown and overrated. I'm sorry he's dead, but I'm not the only one who thought he was a bit of a rogue. I'm saying no more than that.'

* * *

The two detectives sat in DI French's office in Jubilee House, examining the material SOCO had removed from Sir Frank Taylor's room. On a table near the door lay two old-fashioned box files, three scrapbooks, two bundles of letters, each fastened with faded blue tape, some photo albums, and a tin box containing a number of letters written in German. On the DI's desk was a large manila envelope marked by SOCO as 'personal papers'.

The town hall clock struck four and, right on cue, Paul French glanced at his wristwatch and said: 'That clock's two minutes slow.' Glyn gave the expected response. 'Maybe your watch is two minutes fast.'

French tapped the manila envelope and then waved his hand vaguely in the direction of the table near the door.

'All this, Glyn,' he said, 'all so private and intimate, and suddenly it belongs to nobody. The only person it meant anything to is now a corpse in the mortuary. And here we are, picking over the remnants of a life.'

'You're in a very introspective mood today, sir,' offered Glyn.

'Yes. Yes, I must snap out of it. We were up all night with the baby, which tends to produce a kind of general gloom the next day. And then, seeing the body of poor Sir Frank . . . Come on, Glyn, let's start with his personal papers.'

The first document that he slid out of the envelope was a faded letter typed on Home Office notepaper. It was headed 'Naturalization Document' and was dated 10 January 1954.

To whom it may concern,

This is to confirm that the Naturalization Papers of CHAIM JAKOB SHAPIRO, originally a German citizen and then stateless, are lodged at his request with the Aliens Bureau of the Home Office, where they may be consulted by authorized persons. Further, it is confirmed that the said CHAIM JAKOB SHAPIRO has taken the name FRANK TAYLOR, and that this is now his legal name under the Laws of Great Britain and Northern Ireland.

G. Lloyd George. Home Secretary. W.A. Robinson. Bureau Clerk.

'He wasn't naturalized until 1954,' said DI French. 'I wonder why he left it so late? Ah! Here's his original passport.'

The document was heavily stained with water, and what may have been blood. The photograph showed a round-faced boy of fourteen or fifteen, wearing a smart linen jacket, and gazing solemnly at the camera. It was a face that, in its later maturity, would entrance thousands. The name, handwritten in a spiky hand, was clear enough to read: Chaim Jakob Shapiro, but the date, and other handwritten details, had been effectively washed away.

Heavily stamped diagonally across the photograph was the single letter: *J*.

'So there it is,' said French. 'Somehow or other he escaped from that nightmare. We'll send that up to Forensics, to see what they can make of that stain. And they may be able to decipher some of the writing.' He looked back in the box. 'So much for the personal documents — there's hardly anything here.'

'No birth, or marriage, certificate. Sir Frank Taylor seems to have lived a solitary life. Maybe . . .'

'Maybe he lost all his family in the Holocaust?'

'There's something else missing, sir, if Anthony Hayling is to be believed. Do you remember what he said? He told us that Sir Frank had some family snaps, but also pictures of the "Nazi bigwigs". What's happened to them? Are we missing something here?'

'I think there's quite a few things missing . . . Let's see what's in these bundles of letters.'

One envelope contained copies of professional contracts, and the other, a selection of fan mail. The photo albums were much more interesting. They chronicled the glittering career of Sir Frank Taylor from the fifties until his retirement in 1993. There were flash photographs of him leaving various theatres, smilingly signing autographs; more formal shots of him receiving the MBE, the OBE, and finally his knighthood in 1972. Other pictures showed him relaxing on a yacht, skiing in the Alps, opening garden fêtes, enjoying the fruits of his hard-won success. And behind this, half-hidden in the past, the world of a water-sodden, possibly bloodstained, passport, over-stamped in the Nazi era with the single letter: J.

The tin box contained a number of handwritten letters, all in German, bearing the post mark of the Free State of Danzig, and addressed to Herr Alphonse Shapiro at Mannheim, in Baden-Wurttemberg.

'I know a man who will be able to tell us whether that Nazi dagger is genuine or not,' said DI French. 'Wickes thought it might be a replica, but then, he's no expert, and neither am I. But Mervyn Sanders is. He keeps a rather special curio shop near Provost's Lane and was a great help to me a couple of years ago in that Singing Statue business. We'll take the dagger for him to look at tomorrow, and see what he says.'

* * *

'A fake? Oh, no, gentlemen, this dagger is the real thing.'

French and Edwards were standing in the cluttered curio shop of Mervyn Sanders. Mervyn held up the fatal dagger, examined it closely with a jeweller's lens, and then put it down on the shop counter.

'This,' he said, 'is an example of what was called the *Ehrendolch*, or "honour dagger", part of the ceremonial dress of members of the SS. I say "ceremonial", but of course it was a real weapon, and at just about a foot long, a deadly one. And this was used to murder Sir Frank Taylor?'

'It was.'

'You see this black, burnished ebony handle? Just below it you'll see the manufacturer's logo, which tells me that this was an early production — 1933 to 35. You see that Roman numeral? It's a II, which means that it was issued in the Dresden area. There were three numerals: I, for Munich, II for Dresden, and III for Berlin. Look at the blade: it's engraved with the SS motto, *Meine Ehre heisst Treue.*'

'Meaning?'

'"My honour is loyalty." These people perverted the meaning of such noble words to apply to their criminal fantasies. And now, it's been used to murder one of the greatest British actors of the twentieth century. Himmler said that the dagger could be used to avenge wrongs done to other SS members. This is an interesting early example of the honour dagger. Probably worth about £300.'

'It's not for sale, I'm afraid,' said French. 'It's exhibit A in the future trial of the killer of Sir Frank Taylor.'

* * *

Later that day, Glyn sat at a table in the corner of the Grapes, a popular modern pub in the suburb of Vicar's Cross. In a moment, Glenda would call him into the little dining room to enjoy his gammon and chips. No point in going home yet. Sandra would be out tonight and off to her mother's in Southbourne tomorrow.

Glenda brought him his gammon and chips, which he attacked with gusto. Everything at the Grapes tasted good, was well and carefully cooked, and served by cheerful staff like Glenda and her assistant, Kylie.

He felt old and jaded. His sole interest these days was his work, for which he had a natural aptitude. Detective Inspector French was a man in a million, a man who quite unconsciously showed his regard for Glyn in the way he trusted him with every detail of a case and was content to leave him to pursue lines of enquiry on his own initiative. He also acted as a kind of older brother, making sure that Glyn was taking care of himself, and making ill-deserved allowances for his occasionally turning up late and dishevelled for work.

Kylie brought him a tall glass of refreshing lager, and when he had finished his meal he went back into the bar to sit at his usual table, but saw that it was now occupied by a woman whom he knew vaguely. Marie was an attractive woman in her thirties, well-groomed with sad grey eyes. She spoke quietly, and seemed to accept him as someone who, like herself, was enduring the pain of loneliness. She was sitting with a glass of what Glyn knew was a port and lemon in front of her.

'Hi, Glyn,' she said, 'you've not been in here recently.'

'No,' he smiled. 'I've been too busy at work to get out in the evenings.'

She smiled back, and tentatively sipped her drink. 'I've just got a new job, PA to the director of Beckwith's.'

'I'm pleased to hear it,' said Glyn.

How pompous and bloodless he sounded! But then, he had always been a bit wary of Marie. There was a depth of kindliness about her that drew him to her. But she only ever talked of mundane things. She never spoke of a husband who didn't understand her, or a partner with an ugly temper. She never overstepped the mark by asking him too many questions about himself. Neither knew the other's surname. But whenever he came into the Grapes, he looked out for her, and was disappointed if she wasn't there. No, *frustrated* was a better word.

And he had no right to think such things. He was a married man who had made vows that he intended to keep. It would be different if Marie was one of a crowd, so that he could chat to her without raising eyebrows. But she was always alone, and she wore no ring on her finger.

His frustration must have started to show because Marie asked him whether he was all right.

'Yes, yes, I'm fine. It's time I went. Sandra will be wondering where I've got to.'

6. INTO THE DARK

Noel Greenspan stood at the window of his office in Canal Street, reading that morning's edition of the *Oldshire Gazette*. The murder of Sir Frank Taylor occupied the whole of the front page, and promised to spill over on to page 2. It said that Sir Frank Taylor, 94, for some years a resident of Oldminster, had been stabbed to death with a Nazi dagger. Who could have committed such an atrocity on a man who, in his prime, had enthralled the British theatre-going public with his many roles? Cinemagoers, too, would not forget his contributions to the cinematic art.

Would there be anything in it for him? True, the murder was being investigated by Paul French and Glyn Edwards, two first-class officers who both knew him well, but private detective agencies like Greenspan and McArthur could often delve into corners that the police couldn't reach, because they were hide-bound by their own rules of engagement.

The day had decided to mourn in sympathy, and rain glistened on the pavements down below in Canal Street. There was a word for that — for nature mourning the wretched lot of humankind — the pathetic fallacy. He threw the paper down on his desk.

'Chloe!'

The door opened and his business partner came into the room. As always, she was elegantly dressed in a favourite tailored dress, and one of her treasured jackets from Jaeger. Chloe had been with him for seven years, during which time he had trained her in the business; just recently she'd become a partner in their thriving detective agency. She was his eyes and ears, skilled in the arts of eliciting information.

They both pretended that their relationship was entirely professional, but they knew, deep down, that it was more than that. She was a widow. He was divorced. There was something very dignified about being a widow, but being divorced was a kind of failure. People wondered who had been the 'innocent party', as though the anguish of that kind of final separation was the culmination of a battle between good and evil. Life was more subtle than that.

'Chloe,' said Noel Greenspan, 'We have just lost the greatest Macbeth of the age. Like Hamlet's father, he was the victim of "murder most foul". Still, he *was* ninety-four.' He proceeded to quote a few lines from Macbeth, something he was prone to do, much to the amusement of Chloe.

'I wish you hadn't absorbed so much poetry at Oxford,' said Chloe. 'You used to be keen on Eliot, but now I see you've reverted to Shakespeare. Poor old Sir Frank! You're not going to do that bit about an old man being "sans teeth, sans eyes, sans taste, sans everything", are you?'

'I had contemplated it but thought it would be too cruel. I saw him once, Ibsen's *The Master Builder* at the National Theatre. I can still hear and see him now, as he enthralled a packed audience. He always had a slight foreign lilt to his voice, which suited his Ibsen roles. He could suggest Norwegians without forcing the issue.'

'The *Gazette* says that he came to this country in 1945, "as a refugee from war-torn Europe". He was Jewish, apparently. I wonder what country he came from, originally.'

'It also says that his real name was Chaim Jakob Shapiro, but he took the name Frank Taylor when he came to this country. Some quite famous Jewish actors adopted stage names that obscured their origin — that's pretty sad, that they had to do that. Edward G. Robinson was one of them. His real name was Emanuel Goldenberg. He came from Romania originally.'

'So, if Sir Frank was Jewish and stabbed to death with a Nazi dagger . . .' said Chloe.

'Yes, and that makes me wonder—'

At that moment the phone on Greenspan's desk began to ring.

'Hello? Yes, this is Greenspan and McArthur . . . Yes, I've been reading about it in today's paper. You are . . . Oh, Mr Charles Forshaw. What can we do for you? . . . Certainly, you can come any time this morning to suit your convenience . . . Eleven? Yes, that will be fine. I look forward to seeing you then.'

Noel put the phone down and rubbed his hands.

'That was one of the residents of the Irving Home for Retired Actors. He says he's in a quandary, and would value our expert advice.'

* * *

Noel Greenspan looked at the man sitting opposite him at the office desk and thought he looked vaguely familiar. He could be in his eighties, but he was still extremely handsome, with thick grey hair. He was very smart, and well turned out, wearing pressed slacks and a sports jacket. Where had he seen him before?

'This is my business partner, Chloe McArthur,' said Noel. 'What can we do for you, Mr Forshaw?'

Their visitor looked uneasy, and abashed, as though he had done something rather disreputable by venturing into their tidy but clinical office in Canal Street. He had brought a zip-up document case with him, which he had placed on Noel's desk.

'I'm here about Sir Frank Taylor's death,' said Charles Forshaw. He blushed and began to fiddle with his tie. 'I expect you know that he was murdered? It's monstrous! Poor old fellow. What kind of monster murders a ninety-four-year-old man?'

He relapsed into gloomy silence. Whatever the reason for his visit, he was finding it heavy going. Chloe glanced at the clock.

'Would you like a cup of coffee, Mr Forshaw?' she asked. 'After all, it's mid-morning. We brew proper coffee here, you know — Blue Mountain.'

'Well, that would be very nice, thank you. Very civilized, if I may say so.'

'Oh!' cried Noel. 'I've just realized who you are, Mr Forshaw. You were the inventive chauffeur in *Mary Kelly Investigates*, with Diana Rigg!'

Charles Forshaw laughed, and relaxed in his chair.

'I plead guilty, Mr Greenspan! People often think they know me, when in fact they've just seen me on TV more years ago than I care to remember. Now, let me tell you why I've come here today.

'A couple of weeks ago Sir Frank Taylor came to see me in my quarters in the Irving Home for Retired Actors, bringing that document case with him. He told me he didn't have very long to live — not because of his age, but because he had inoperable cancer. I began to say how sorry I was, but he cut me short. "I have enemies, Charles," he said. These enemies from his days in Germany were determined to kill him for what they regard as crimes that he committed against them. He'd just learned that one of them had come looking for him here, in Oldminster.

'I asked him whether he had informed the police, but he said it was not a matter for them at all. It was something that belonged to the past. "I have a strong premonition that I will be murdered," Frank said. And he told me he wanted his killers brought to justice, either here in England, or abroad.

'And then he told me that in the event of his being murdered, he wanted you — Greenspan and McArthur — to carry out an investigation and find the killers.'

'Well, that's a remarkable story, Mr Forshaw,' said Noel Greenspan, 'but I'm afraid—'

'I was to give you this cheque,' said Forshaw, reaching into an inside pocket. 'He showed it to me, and as you'll, see, it's made out to you, but the sum has been left blank. You'll see that he's written across the top, "Not to exceed twenty-five thousand pounds."'

After an awed silence, Noel spoke. 'I should be very happy to take the case, Mr Forshaw,' he said. 'And this document wallet contains some evidence?'

'As far as I can make out, that document case contains a random collection of things that Frank had amassed over the years. He told me that it would be a start, something that an intelligent man like yourself would be able to make good use of. You were recommended to him by a titled gentleman. He wouldn't say who it was.'

The look of embarrassment had returned.

'I thought it was all nonsense, but when it actually happened, I found myself in a quandary. By rights, all this should go to the police. They already have a pile of documents and other stuff from Frank's desk, and that document case should be with them. But I promised Frank: he and I really were friends, you know, and of course I revered him for his wonderful life and career.'

'If we find anything that should be given to the police,' said Noel, 'then we will surrender it to Inspector French at Jubilee House. Thank you for coming in today, Mr Forshaw. We'll keep you posted as our investigation progresses.'

When Forshaw had gone, Noel unzipped the document case and carefully slid its contents on to the desk. There was a small photo album, secured with a perishing elastic band, and a number of yellowing letters, some still in their envelopes. There were some objects lodged in the bottom of the case. Noel shook them out. There was a gold swastika suspended from a delicate gold chain, a pair of diamond earrings, and a set of Nazi cap and shoulder badges. Souvenirs? Perhaps.

'What do you make of these?' Noel asked Chloe.

'I think a lot of German women wore those pendants,' she answered, 'much like many people today wear iconography. But why Sir Frank should have them, I can't imagine. And these badges — they've got the death's-head on them, so they were probably part of someone's SS uniform.'

'Like the dagger that was used to murder him,' said Noel. 'They could be souvenirs — or trophies, more likely. If Sir Frank — no, let's call him Chaim Jakob Shapiro in this context — if Chaim escaped from a concentration camp, he may have had to kill a guard in order to do so. They were different times, desperate times . . .'

'Let's look at the photographs first,' said Chloe. 'There's some truth in the old adage that "a picture's worth a thousand words".'

All the photographs were in black-and-white, and were clearly home snaps taken with a simple box camera. They had all been glued into the album, which was backed in cardboard covered with a patterned paper. They were mainly family groups, showing a man and woman posing with a boy in the back garden of their house. They were all smiling and the clothes showed that the pictures had been taken in the early thirties.

'Do you think that could be Chaim with his parents?' asked Noel. 'He looks about ten in those three photos, and nearer twelve or thirteen in the later ones.'

'It could be, I suppose. But if you look at the woman through this lens, you'll see that she's wearing a swastika necklace. I suppose it could be Chaim.'

'Talk about political differences!' Noel whistled. 'Could she have been a gentile — and married Mr Shapiro, a Jew? I suppose it's not entirely impossible. Especially if these pictures predate the bigoted Nuremberg Laws . . .'

'Or they may be photographs of friends or relatives. What a pity that there are no captions! They're all taken in the same garden. That's a linden tree against the fence, and you can see one of those tall church steeples common in Germany. I wonder where they were taken?'

She means the photographs, thought Noel, *but my question is, where were this man, this woman and this child taken?*

He moved to the window, and looked down into Canal Street. A dark cloud had temporarily blotted out the sun. All these pictures of ordinary folk in pre-war Germany were shadowed with the knowledge that so many of them faced an unimaginable fate. No house, no home, no garden with a linden tree for them.

Noel Greenspan jerked himself back into the present. Chloe was telling him something.

'Here's another photograph, a glossy professional one, I think. It shows Hitler, standing in front of a building — it looks like a museum. He's in civilian clothes, and he's posing with Hermann Goering and Josef Goebbels. Somebody's written in pencil here, on a blank page near the back of the album. It looks like a child's writing, and — Oh! It's in English. "Our house in Kaiser Wilhelm Strasse, Leipzig. Me with Mummy and Daddy. May 1934. This book belongs to Franz Schneider, aged 10. Heil Hitler!"'

'So, it's not Chaim,' said Noel. 'Probably friends or relations? I wonder why the boy wrote that in English?' He moved back to the desk. 'We'd better have a look at the letters. They all look a bit faded and tatty, but here's a more recent one, postmarked the twentieth of October last year. It's addressed to Sir Frank Taylor at the Irving Home for Retired Actors, and it's from somebody called Dom Edgar Hughes, a monk at St Anselm's Priory in Cricklewood.' He began to read the letter aloud. '"Dear Sir Frank," it says, "I received a request from the Prior of Kloster Eisenbach, in Germany, to forward the enclosed letter unopened to you. I have great pleasure in doing so." Short and to the point.'

'Is the enclosed letter still there?'

'No. I expect it's somewhere in this pile of documents on the desk. Yes, here it is.'

Noel picked up the letter. It was evidently old, headed with a little sepia engraving of an onion-domed church and other buildings clinging to a hillside followed by some faded printed words: 'Kloster Eisenbach, in Rheinland-Pfalz'. 'The letter itself is in English,' he said, surprised. 'Just like that boy Franz's inscription in the photograph album.

> *Dear friend, I know for certain that one at least of them is already in England. Prepare yourself, if you can. They will not consider your age when they come to extract vengeance. The motto is still, Meine Ehre heisst Treue.*

He looked up at Chloe. 'I wonder what that means? I wish Lance Middleton was here. There's not a language he doesn't know. The letter ends *Gott mit uns,* and is signed "Anselm", with the letters KH in brackets after it.'

'So that's the letter that Sir Frank received,' said Chloe. 'The letter Charles Forshaw told us about, warning him that some unnamed people were on his track. This is going to be our way in, Noel.' She glanced back down at the pile of letters and photographs. 'What else have we got here?'

A brittle cellophane envelope contained a photograph of a British Army officer, his shoulder badges showing the three pips of a captain. On the back was written: *A memento for Herr Shapiro, from your friend Captain Mark Rogers, R.A.S.C.* It was accompanied by a typed letter, headed HQ BAOR Hamburg, commending Chaim Jakob Shapiro as an intelligent and reliable worker, who spoke perfect English, as well as his native German. It was a valuable reference, presumably offering a lifeline to a stateless person after the war.

'Here's something quite different,' said Chloe, who had been sifting through the remaining letters. 'It's from a man called John Brassington, importer, at an address in Birmingham, and dated the fifth of April 1948.

> *'Look here, Chaim, I won't wait much longer. I was very good to you, and helped you to set yourself up on your own. But you still owe me £500. If you don't pay this debt soon, cash or cheque, I'll send a couple of men round to rearrange your handsome features.*

'And so it goes on. Chaim, or Frank Taylor, as he became, once worked for some company or other in Birmingham. We need to look into that, too.'

Noel turned the letter over, and saw that someone had written in ink: 'Got Mr Friedlander to send him a solicitor's letter, telling him to back off. I'll pay him when I'm able.'

There were a number of receipts from charities, including one in Berlin specializing in the support of aged and destitute Jews. A letter from the Danzig Old Comrades Association, written in German, acknowledged receipt of a banker's draft for £1,000. It was dated 17 August 1950.

'What do you make of it all?' asked Chloe. 'It's a tangled web, and no mistake. But the way in, as I said, is that letter from the priest at Cricklewood.'

'I'll go up to town tomorrow,' said Noel, 'and see what I can find out. You remember Peter Hamilton at the Foreign Office? There are a few questions I might like to ask him, and while I'm there I'll see if I can catch Lance Middleton at Lincoln's Inn. We need to photocopy all these documents, and take the originals to the police at Jubilee House. We'll hang on to the photo album.'

Chloe went into the next room, switched on the photocopier, and began the task of duplicating Sir Frank Taylor's hoard of letters and documents. Noel Greenspan stood at the window, once more looking down at the bleak prospect of Canal Street. It had started to rain again. The atmosphere in the office seemed to have been stifled and oppressed by the memories of the Nazi era, by the photographs of people who, one way or another, may have been doomed to annihilation either in the Nazi camps, or in the gulags of the victors. What had happened to Sir Frank Taylor when he was a young man — little more than a boy — in the dying days of Hitler's Germany? How had he survived to transform himself into one of England's greatest actors, a revered establishment figure?

A strange feeling of uncertainty began to creep into his mind. How much of all this was fact, and how much fancy? Why had Sir Frank Taylor been murdered? It would be criminally irresponsible not to share their findings with DI French and DS Edwards at Jubilee House. It wasn't enough to erect theories of what may have happened both in the past and at the present time without some sober and reliable facts upon which to base an investigation. He recalled how Macbeth had become the victim of his fatal indecision:

. . . function is smothered in surmise, and nothing is, but what is not.

* * *

Bosszuallo sat hunched over the keyboard, in a room illuminated only by the pale blue light of the monitor. He was safe up here — safe from prying eyes and listening ears. It was in the dark hours of the night, between two and four o'clock, that he was able to separate Bosszuallo from his other, conflicting identity, and put what was left of his disintegrating mind to the task in hand.

Armed with the secrecy of the Tor browser, Bosszuallo trawled the dark web until he found the new website of Msciciel. There was news posted there of fresh missions launched in Russia and Bulgaria, where willing hands had been found to continue the work of vengeance. There were already some messages waiting for him to read, one from Msciciel himself.

Your work is over. You have avenged all the blood that Frank Taylor shed. Do not call it murder. It was an execution.

The other messages were in the same vein.

So all Franz Schneider's victims could finally rest in peace.

Here were the headaches again, the blurred vision, the voices whispering endlessly inside his head. Growing louder by the minute. He knew he needed to rest, sleep, blot it out.

Blotted out from the Book of Life. It was murder, insisted the insidious voice now screaming inside his head, battering at the doors of his perception. *It was murder. You went out into the night, and stabbed him to the heart.*

Bosszuallo staggered to his bed, and wrestled for some dire time with the agony of migraine before he fell asleep through sheer exhaustion.

* * *

The following morning, a Tuesday, found Noel Greenspan in the north London district of Cricklewood, where he made his way to a quiet cul-de-sac near Gladstone Park. Here he found St Anselm's Priory, a fanciful red-brick Victorian building standing in half an acre of gardens. He was admitted by an elderly monk in the black habit of the Benedictines, who took the business card that was offered him and conducted Noel to a comfortably furnished room that he took to be the visitors' parlour. In a few moments he was joined by Dom Edgar Hughes, an impressive grey-haired man in his fifties. Like the monk who had admitted him, he wore the black habit of his order, with the cowl thrown back to reveal his muscular neck. Noel, who had played rugby at Oxford, wondered whether Dom Edgar had been a prop forward in his youth.

'Sit down, Mr Greenspan,' said Dom Edgar. 'I'm the sub-prior here. I see from your card that you're a private detective. What can I do for you? Have any of my brethren been misbehaving?'

'Not to my knowledge, sir,' said Noel, smiling. 'I've come because I was engaged by the late Sir Frank Taylor to investigate his death. Of course, he engaged me to do so before he was murdered . . . It would be less confusing if I were to tell you the whole story.'

When he had finished, he produced a set of photocopies from a folder, and handed them to the sub-prior.

'There's an unpleasant whiff of Nazism about all this business,' he said. 'It's clear that Sir Frank Taylor was a Jewish escapee from a concentration camp, and that for reasons at present unknown some shadowy figures from the Nazi era were after his blood. As you will have seen in the papers, sir, they were only too successful in murdering that poor old man. He was ninety-four.'

'You have lodged the originals of these papers with the police? It's imperative that they should see that letter from Kloster Eisenbach. "Kloster", you know, is the German variant of our word "cloister", meaning "priory". Let's see what we can find out about Eisenbach Priory.'

Dom Edgar crossed the room, and opened a glazed bookcase, from which he took a large, leather-bound volume.

'This is a sort of Benedictine *Who's Who*,' he said. He began to flick through the pages. 'Ah! Here we are. Kloster Eisenbach, founded 1465 in Eisenbach, a small hill town in what is now the Rhineland-Palatinate. Very nice . . . That's a very romantic and picturesque part of Germany. I've been to Mainz, but never to Eisenbach. The priory's famed for its extensive vineyards, and does a lively trade as a vintner, selling primarily to the German market — or so it says here.'

'And this man who signs himself Anselm,' said Noel. 'What can you tell me about him?'

'Well, Mr Greenspan, Anselm's a very popular name for Benedictine monks — after St Anselm, one of the great figures of our order. Evidently, this person was a friend of Sir Frank Taylor's from his youthful days, and knew about some impending threat to his life. He puts the letters "KH" after his name. They're probably his real initials, suggesting that Sir Frank knew him long before he became a monk. That's just an idea. I may be wrong.'

Dom Edgar finished reading the entry in the reference book.

'It says that they also have a medical wing at Kloster Eisenbach,' he said, 'where aged and ailing monks from all over Germany can be looked after. It's by way of being a particular charism — power — of the place.' He began to look thoughtful, and troubled.

'I wonder . . .' He began, and then stopped.

'I know,' said Noel. 'Perhaps this Anselm was another fugitive who found safety in the cloister, another frail man in his nineties, who might be next on the list. He quoted something in German in his letter to Sir Frank. Can you tell me what it means?'

'*Meine Ehre heisst Treue.* It means, "My honour is loyalty".' He looked up at Noel. 'It was the motto of the SS.'

* * *

Peter Hamilton occupied a cramped set of rooms in the rear of the Foreign Office building, affording him a tantalizing view of a corner of St James's Park. He sat at a plain wooden table, surrounded by tall green metal filing cabinets. On the table was a rather chunky computer and a battery of telephones.

'I'd like to say that you haven't changed since our Oxford days, Noel,' he said, 'but I mustn't tell fibs. You're — well, more solid, if you know what I mean.'

Noel laughed. 'We're neither of us sylphlike these days,' he said. 'But I'm sure that our gain in weight has been matched by an increase in wisdom.'

Hamilton grinned. 'Shall we have some coffee? I can spare you a few minutes. And I'm sure you won't say no to a biscuit.' With some effort, he hefted himself from his chair and exited the room. Minutes later, he returned, carrying a cup in each hand. 'From our vending machine.' He handed one cup to Noel, then set about rummaging in his desk. 'Now, I know I have some biscuits left somewhere in here . . .'

'You're looking positively glowing,' said Noel wryly, just as Hamilton produced a near-empty pack of Rich Teas. 'Nice pinstripe suit and Harrow tie.' He clapped his hands together. 'Now that the formalities are over, I want you to look at some photocopies of documents that are in some way connected with the murder of Sir Frank Taylor, the distinguished actor.'

Noel took a sip of his coffee and set it down quickly — he was no fan of vending-machine stuff. The Rich Tea biscuits were stale. He watched his old friend as he looked carefully through the photocopies.

'Frank Taylor's death was appalling,' said Peter Hamilton. 'Even now, when we're inured to violence, it was particularly revolting. But these documents . . . There's nothing here that the FO could help you with. The only thing—'

One of the phones interrupted him with its strident ring.

'Hamilton. What? No, he's in Beijing all week, and then straight on to Berlin. I'm not at liberty to discuss it just now. Do call again tomorrow, won't you?' He put the phone down, and scribbled something on a note pad.

'The only thing,' he said, continuing as if the phone call hadn't happened, 'is that charity, the Danzig Old Comrades' Association, which Sir Frank sent a donation of £1,000 to. We know something about that — something that Sir Frank could not have known about. It was a haven just after the war for various minor Nazi officials, who were given all kinds of aid — new identities, forged papers, things like that. I don't suppose it's like that now, but the German internal security people still keep an eye on it.'

*　*　*

Lance Middleton was sitting at his little round dining table in the panelled office of his chambers in Lincoln's Inn. As always when eating, he had a napkin tucked under his ample chin. Everything about Lance Middleton, QC, was ample. Chloe had once sent him some slimming menus, which he had never acknowledged.

'Sit down, Noel,' said Lance, raising a morsel of fish to his mouth. 'I'll be with you in a few moments. Have a glass of this Moselle. It's good of its type, not arrogant, but not shy or retiring, either.'

Noel knew his way around his old friend's chambers. He located a suitable glass, and poured himself some wine. He recalled Peter Hamilton's vile coffee, and wondered how such a decent man could put up with it.

'What are you eating? It looks great.'

'This is a sole *bonne femme*, a reminder of the glory days of real French cuisine. There's a little café round the corner from here that'll send things in for you, if you're prepared to pay the extortionate price. So, what have you brought me?'

Noel told him the whole story of Sir Frank Taylor, his murder, his antecedents, and the cache of documents that the old actor had entrusted to his care. He had brought the photograph album with him, and he added this to the pile of photocopies. Lance moved to his cluttered desk, the adipose gourmet replaced by the earnest lawyer.

'The last time I delved into documents for you,' said Lance at length, 'I ended up making some innocent — or fairly innocent — people very unhappy,' he said. 'If I go digging around in this lot, am I going to harm anyone still living?'

'You might uncover a particularly callous murderer.'

'Well, maybe. What's your motivation here?'

'Sir Frank Taylor had left me a cheque for services rendered, not to exceed twenty-five thousand pounds.'

'Hmm . . . he asked you to investigate his death? He knew he'd likely be murdered?' When Noel nodded, Lance looked back down at the papers in front of him. 'Odd that. Why didn't he go to the police? These documents — there's a curious aura of Englishness about them, isn't there? The old German monk writes in good English. But then, many well-educated Germans do. The little German boy also writes in English, and talks about "Mummy" and "Daddy". There they are in the photograph, a couple of smiling blondes, the lady wearing a swastika necklace. Franz Schneider, aged ten. Significant, don't you think? Maybe little Franz's father was German and his mother was English.'

'What's so significant about Franz Schneider?'

'Well, translate it into English. Franz means Frank. And Schneider is German for tailor. Frank Taylor.'

'You mean—'

'I don't mean anything yet, Noel. I'm just thinking aloud in my usual manner. Skirting the earthworks. I'll do what I can for you, but you must leave these copies with me, and also the photo album. I'm due to visit Strasbourg on EU business, so I'll go this week, provided that you agree to "all expenses paid". I've heard of Kloster Eisenbach and its celebrated vintages. I could turn my visit into a little holiday.'

'They've something else there at Kloster Eisenbach,' said Noel, 'a sort of infirmary for ancient monks, and one of them is the mysterious Brother Anselm. Exercise your skills in German by talking to him. Unless, of course, he turns out to be English.'

7. THE FADED WREATH

On Wednesday morning, 25 April, five days after the murder of Sir Frank, DI French and DS Edwards were able to interview George Cavanagh, the house manager, who had returned from his stay with Bishop Poindexter at Oldminster Palace. As usual, French was there some time before Edwards, who shot in just as the interview was starting with an uncharacteristic look of excitement on his face.

Cavanagh glanced at the clock impatiently. He was a tall, rangy man in his fifties, his long face showing the heavy blue shadow of a potential beard and moustache desperate to be liberated from the morning razor. He had slightly prominent teeth, which caused him to struggle with a slight lisp.

'I know nothing about this affair, gentlemen,' he said, 'because of course I wasn't here. Sir Frank was one of our resident treasures. I didn't know him well, I spend most of my time ensuring that this place runs efficiently and gives value for money, but yes, Sir Frank's demise is a bitter blow to us all.'

George Cavanagh was wearing a smart sage-green suit, a pristine white shirt and a red tie. He sat back in the chair behind his desk in his neat office, glancing occasionally at his large gold wristwatch. *He doesn't give a damn about Frank*

Taylor, Glyn thought. *This is a man who measures worth in pounds and pence.* The notoriety of a murder might well unsettle the financial integrity of the Irving Home.

'I expect you know he was Jewish?' said Cavanagh. 'Frank Taylor wasn't his real name. Perhaps he fell victim to some neo-Nazi thug.'

DS Edwards bit back a terse reply. *Anything but admit that the old actor's killer was someone nearer home.* Still, he had to admit Cavanagh's theory wasn't beyond the realms of possibility.

'Well, you see, Mr Cavanagh,' said DI French, 'we've made very thorough enquiries and inspections, and it's quite certain that nobody broke into the home on the night of Sir Frank's murder. No neo-Nazis, or people of that sort. We're worried it was an inside job.'

George Cavanagh waved away an inside job.

'No, no, Inspector, it's not possible. You've seen the CCTV footage and that would have shown you that the house was secure. But have you considered that a would-be assassin could have concealed himself on the premises earlier in the day? There are constant comings and goings here — delivery vans, visitors, people who come to entertain the residents — all sorts. There are extensive cellars under the house where a determined killer could conceal himself.' Cavanagh warmed to his subject. 'And then there are the attics — all sorts of places. And after he had crept out and committed the murder, what could have been easier than to leave the house when all the commotion began? Nurse Trickett told me that the place was in an uproar.'

DS Edwards was about to say something, but French silenced him with a look. Cavanagh's suggestions sounded logical, until you considered that Trudy never left reception without calling someone to cover her; anyone coming into the building even in daylight hours needed to be buzzed in or have an access key. Trudy, he thought, was the noticing type — not someone who would lose sight of a stranger on her turf. Even so, he thought with a chill, Wickes and the team of SOCOs wouldn't have searched the cellars.

'Well, thank you very much for your suggestions, Mr Cavanagh,' said French. 'It's always useful to have a fresh angle on things. Now, we have already interviewed the residents, and most of the domestic staff. But there's the nursing staff that we're anxious to talk to, and we'd be very grateful if you could arrange for us to see them for a few minutes this morning. Before I do so, could you tell me if any of the staff live in?'

'Certainly. Nurse Trickett has a ground-floor flat at the back of the house, so in a manner of speaking she's always on duty. Teddy Balonek, the cook, has a small flat in the attic storey. Our gardener, Terry Lucas, lives in the lodge at the gate. Everybody else, including myself, lives out. My house is in Cathedral Walk, just a few minutes away from here. All the nurses live out.'

'Thank you very much for that information, Mr Cavanagh,' said French. He added, 'My colleague and I are very impressed with the general air of efficiency here. I rather gather that it originates from you!'

Steady on, guvnor! thought DS Edwards. *Don't overdo it, or he'll think you're taking the mickey. Which, of course, you are.*

The house manager blushed with pleasure.

'That's very kind of you to say so, Inspector. Now, I know the nurses are keen to talk to you while they're all here together at the change of shift? They're waiting outside. I'll make myself scarce until you're done.'

Before the inspector could reply, the nurses were through the door and Cavanagh was shuffling out — they ran a tight ship here, and it seemed the police would have to fit to the same timetable. Jean Buckley and Mary Helm were in their twenties, smartly dressed in nurses' uniform, and clearly capable, though slightly subdued by the presence of the two police officers. Gabriel Swift was older, but like his colleagues smartly dressed and confident. All three responded readily to French's questions.

Sir Frank was suffering from terminal prostate cancer and would have lived no more than a further two or three months. No, it was a form of the disease that didn't cause

74

much pain, though he was regularly sedated with controlled quantities of morphine. Yes, all three had treated him. He often talked to them about his great days, and the people he'd met. He knew his end was near but reckoned that ninety-four was a good innings.

'Did he ever suggest that an enemy was threatening him, someone connected with his early days in Germany?'

DI French saw Gabriel glance at the others as though seeking their consent to tell him something.

'One morning, when things were a bit difficult for him, he said to me: "Swift, I may be dead before this cancer gets me. There's a devil from the past who's begun stalking me, and I wouldn't be surprised if he doesn't get to me before the Grim Reaper." I told him he should let the police know but he said it'd be no good, that they couldn't do anything. "These things run deep," he said, "hidden for decades. Deep vengeance." He seemed quite resigned. I remember him saying he'd take whatever fate threw at him.'

'What did you make of that?'

'Well, you've got to take everything these actors say with a pinch of salt. They make things up, or you think they're telling you something when in fact they're quoting from some old play. So I didn't pay much attention to what he said. I'm sorry I didn't now, because it turns out he was right all the time. It seems that someone from his past was able to get to him.'

'He used to have dreams,' Jean added. 'He'd cry out, and thrash around in his bed, frail as he was. I'd hear him when I was on night duty. He'd be shouting out in German, and when I woke him up to settle his pillows he'd carry on speaking in German, even though I didn't understand a word. But he was usually a kind, nice old man, generous with gifts for the staff at Christmas. Things like that. I'm not a theatregoer, but I know that he was a famous stage actor. I'm very sorry he's dead.'

'Thanks for that.' DI French cleared his throat. 'Is there anything you want to add, Sergeant Edwards?'

'Only that Sir Frank was stabbed to death with a Nazi dagger,' said Glyn. 'Did any of you ever see it? We've had it checked and it's not a replica. This is the real thing. We were told that Mr Hayling may have had such a dagger in his room.'

Once again, the three nurses seemed to seek each other's permission to speak.

'That dagger belonged to Sir Frank,' said Mary Helm. 'He kept it in a wooden box in the top drawer of his bureau. I thought it was a prop from one of his plays. He had a lot of souvenirs once, but he gave them away to some theatrical museum in London.'

'But Mr Hayling—'

'Mr Hayling is a kleptomaniac,' said Mary Helm, blushing. 'Poor old man, he can't help it, and for the most part doesn't know that he's lifting things from his friends' rooms. If we spot something's gone missing, we can retrieve it from his room and quietly return it. Most of the others know about it, and nobody much minds. Poor Mr Hayling, he's had so much to put up with in his life.' The nurse's eyes filled with tears and she excused herself suddenly from the room.

'Mary's very fond of Mr Hayling,' said Gabriel.

'I can't think why,' said Jean hotly. 'He was involved in a call-girl scandal that cost him his career. Mary's just being silly.'

'Thank you very much for your time,' French said, using Mary's exit as a good time to wrap up the interview. 'We'll be in touch if anything else comes up.' When the two nurses had left the room, he turned to Glyn. 'So that's it. Tracey Potter was right when she told us that she'd seen the dagger in Hayling's room, but she evidently knew nothing about his kleptomania. So the dagger was Frank Taylor's all along. A Nazi dagger kept as a souvenir by a Holocaust survivor.'

'My granddad had a cigarette lighter with a swastika on it,' said Glyn. 'He took it from the dead body of a German soldier at Arnhem.'

'Yes . . . And I can well imagine how such things happen in the heat of war. But I mustn't ramble, Glyn — I know

76

you're itching to get back to that pile of papers that Noel Greenspan dropped off at the station.'

'Very funny, sir,' said Edwards, producing a paper from his pocket. 'You've noticed that I've been bursting to show you this since I got here. Those papers have given us a lead.'

The paper in question was a copy of a letter from someone called John Brassington, written to Sir Frank Taylor when he was still Chaim Jakob Shapiro, a lifetime ago, in 1948, demanding the sum of £500 to be repaid in full.

French gave the letter back to him. 'Great work, Glyn. But aren't we looking for a more recent creditor? Let's keep this in mind, but you need to keep going through those papers from Greenspan.'

Edwards didn't suppress his groan. Most of the papers so far were closely written notes on stagecraft, interspersed with shopping lists, and each one had to be read carefully and then logged, however irrelevant.

'Let's finish these interviews,' went on French, as if he hadn't heard him. 'We won't bring the others here. Let's talk to them on their own ground. There's the receptionist, Trudy Vosper, and the PA, Cathy Billington.'

* * *

Trudy Vosper, a small blonde woman clad in a black trouser suit and frilly white shirt, stood behind her desk in reception, and rapidly weighed up her visitors. The inspector didn't look like a policeman. With his carefully brushed thinning hair and prim rimless glasses, he could have passed for one of those office-bound clerks in a job centre. But she knew it was he who'd solved the murder at Renfield Hall last year, and he was said to be very clever.

'So there you are, Inspector,' said Trudy Vosper. 'All the duplicate keys to the guests' rooms are kept in this locked key-cupboard. There are three keys to open it. I have one, Mrs Billington — she's the PA — has one, and the third is held by Mr Cavanagh. The guests, of course, have their own keys.'

'How about keys to the main doors? I mean the front door, and the door at the rear of the house.'

'All members of staff have a Yale key to the front door, and a mortise key to the back door lock. At night, both these doors are locked and bolted from the inside at ten o'clock.'

'Is there a visitor's book?'

For answer, Trudy produced a black-bound loose-leaf book from a drawer.

'Anyone who calls at the house must sign themselves in and out in this book. There's also a visitor's book over there on that table, for people to write nice things about the Irving Home.' She smiled, revealing even but rather over-white teeth.

French looked at the reception book and pointed to an entry. 'This one hasn't signed out, on the night of the 20th.'

'No,' sniffed Trudy. 'That was the evening speaker, Mr Sanders. Charles Forshaw let him out. The residents are supposed to get them to sign out, but most of them forget.' French could see it was a long-running grievance for Trudy Vosper that the residents didn't appreciate her filing system.

'Miss Vosper,' said DS Edwards, 'what would I have to do if I wanted to go down to the cellars?'

'The cellars? No unauthorized persons are allowed in the cellars — they house the boilers and the central heating plant. Keys to the cellars are held by myself, Mr Cavanagh, and Terry Lucas. Terry keeps his tools and suchlike down there.'

Not for the first time DI French felt genuine admiration for the way the Irving Home for Retired Actors was run — mostly thanks to this one efficient woman, it seemed.

* * *

'Life here's very predictable, Inspector,' said Cathy.

A middle-aged woman in a neatly tailored suit, she looked at the two detectives over half-moon reading glasses attached to a neck-chain. She exuded a faint aroma of scent and tobacco, and French noted that her fingers were nicotine-stained. Again, routine questions evinced ready answers. In her own tidy office with its Mac glowing on its own desk, she was very close to the top echelon of the Irving Home's management team.

'Has there ever been any scandal here, Mrs Billington?' asked Glyn Edwards.

'*Scandal?*' She laughed. 'No, there's been no scandal, though we have a few scandalous residents here. Actors, you know, are a volatile race.'

Then she bit her lip, and Glyn saw that fresh tears had welled up in eyes that were already red-rimmed. Something was amiss.

'No, there's no scandal here, Sergeant,' she said at last. 'But we've— You've spoken to Mr Cavanagh, haven't you? He's a very good man, and prominent in cathedral circles. But he's a big softie. "Give a man a second chance," all that kind of thing. Well, I don't approve of it myself. So, you might want to look beyond the confines of the house, and poke around in the garden. You'll find a gardener there, Terry Lucas. Maybe you should look him up in one of your databases at Jubilee House.' Cathy dabbed her eyes.

'You think this Terry—'

'I don't think anything, Inspector. I'm just making a suggestion.' She blushed suddenly, but then her tone darkened. 'But that man could have been the way in for an intruder. Flash him a wad of notes, and he'd be yours.'

As the detectives left Cathy's office, French murmured to his colleague: 'Well, that was all pretty damning, wasn't it?'

'Yes. Evidently Cathy thinks Mr Cavanagh employs prisoners on release,' Glyn replied, 'and she doesn't approve.'

* * *

The body of Sir Frank Taylor was released for burial on Thursday 26 April, and the great and the good began to jostle for position. The distinguished actor seemed to have had no particular base during his glory years. He had lived in various rented houses in London's Mayfair, and for a time had occupied an expensive apartment in Clarence Gate, but though a nominal Anglican, he had never attended a parish church, or indeed bothered much with religion.

It had not been difficult, even so, for the Lord Mayor of Oldminster and Bishop Poindexter to secure the honour of burying Sir Frank Taylor in the cemetery at St Thomas of Canterbury — an elegant old church a mere stone's throw from the cathedral — on Wednesday 2 May, the funeral to be followed by a lavish buffet at Oldminster Guildhall. A memorial service would be held in the late summer at St Paul's, Covent Garden, which would be tacitly understood to be a showcase for those modern actors who wished to flaunt their credentials and their wardrobes.

'We'd better attend the funeral, Glyn,' said French. 'We can keep our eyes open for sinister strangers, on the assumption that murderers often turn up at their victims' funerals.'

'Don't you think that's just an old wives' tale?'

'Maybe so, but it does happen, and there'll be a massive turnout, so our killer could easily be lost in the crowd. Now, did you find anything on our gardener friend, Terry Lucas?'

'I did. He's got form, as Mrs Billington hinted. He served a month in prison in 2012 for stealing a few thousand cigarettes from a warehouse. He got six months for breaking and entering in 2014 — incidentally, he attacked the same warehouse as before, still after cigarettes. He always behaved himself in prison, and when he was released from Lea Hill the governor had a word with George Cavanagh, and got him a job as gardener at the Irving Home, where he's since worked really hard, apparently.'

'Let's go and pay a visit to this Terry,' said DI French. 'He sounds like one of those men who flogs contraband in pubs for a few quid, but he may be more. At the moment he's the Irving Home's resident villain, so we need to let him know that we've got our eye on him.'

They found Terry Lucas planting a bush in the strip of garden adjoining the south side of the Irving Home for

Retired Actors. Clad in jeans and T-shirt, he proved to be a well-made, handsome man in his thirties, with a crop of chestnut curls and piercing blue eyes. He seemed completely unfazed by their questions.

'Yes, detectives, I've done time, and paid my debt to society. I wondered whether you'd come to talk to me after poor old Sir Frank was murdered, but I had nothing to do with it.'

There's nothing impertinent or truculent about him, thought Glyn Edwards. He spoke frankly, without any whining or attempts at ingratiation. Still, a few more questions wouldn't go amiss.

'Where were you on the night of the murder, Mr Lucas? The twentieth of April, it was, as I'm sure you'll remember.'

'I was in the Throstle's Nest in Palmerston Square, just round the corner from here. I left about eleven, and went straight home. When I came in from the lodge next morning, I heard the news about Sir Frank.'

'I believe you have a key to the cellars?'

'What? Yes, I do. I keep all my tools down there, even the mowers. It's a faff to lift them down there, but still . . . I used to have a garden shed, and it was broken into. The cellar's more secure.'

Terry suddenly frowned, and they both saw the angry man beneath the reasonable exterior.

'I suppose it was Mrs Bloody Billington who told you that, wasn't it? Managed to make it sound like I was up to no good down there?' he asked. 'Yes, I can see from your expressions that it was our Cathy. Well, the reason she did that, detectives, was because . . . Do you know, I couldn't even tell you. But the woman took against me from the start. Thinks she's a cut above the likes of me, does Widow Billington.'

'Indeed,' French replied coolly. 'Well, thanks you for your time, Mr Lucas.' There was nothing more to get out of this man. He turned to leave, gesturing for his sergeant to accompany him, but Glyn Edwards wasn't there.

DS Edwards had taken advantage of Terry's momentary distraction to walk round the side of the house until he came to a flight of steps leading down to a small bricked area in front of the cellar door. The door was covered with steel sheeting, and when he shook the handle, it remained firm. The little yard — it was no more than four feet square — was littered with cigarette ends. Evidently, this was a favourite place for staff — and possibly guests — to indulge their craving for nicotine. Glyn crouched down and examined his find. Some of the cigarettes had been smoked right down to the filter, others were only half smoked before being stamped out. Some were stained with lipstick. And two of them were the remains of cannabis joints.

As he turned back to meet the guvnor, he decided to make the cellars and their contents a little project of his own. There was obviously more going on here than met the eye.

* * *

The church of St Thomas of Canterbury was packed to the doors for the funeral of Sir Frank Taylor. All the great names of contemporary theatre were there, and most of them had paused before the battery of press cameras waiting for them at the imposing medieval gate that led into the grounds. Lord Bruce-Garden, the impresario and stager of lavish musicals was there with his wife, the actor Dame Margaret Hughes, fresh from her fact-finding tour of Africa.

The front pews, where at most funerals the deceased's family sat, were occupied by the staff and guests of the Irving Home for Retired Actors. Charles Forshaw looked grave and thoughtful. Anthony Hayling fiddled with his walking-stick and looked around the church with evident disapproval. The others contrived to merge into the sea of mourners. At the end of the first pew on the north side, Nurse Trickett sat, guarding her charges.

It was only when the funeral was over, and Sir Frank's coffin had been lowered into the ground, that something untoward happened. As the mourners lingered in the graveyard, admiring and reading the many floral and written tributes to the greater actor, a ripple of disapproval went through the crowd. A man in a dark overcoat and peaked cap muttered, 'Well, that's not very nice! Not what I'd call in the best of taste.' A few people gathered round, and he showed them a wreath that seemed to be composed entirely of faded flowers. Attached to it was a card, upon which was written in block letters a single word: *MÖRDER*.

'What does it mean?' someone asked.

'Well,' said the man in the cap, 'it's German, and it means "MURDERER".'

* * *

Meanwhile, Teddy Balonek had made his own way to the church, but gratefully accepted a lift from George Cavanagh back to the Irving Home. He had dreaded the thought of attending the funeral, knowing it was sure to bring a wave of bad memories washing back over him — deaths he'd experienced in his own family, generations ago in Poland. He would always be plagued with guilt and remorse for the dark deeds of the Baloneks.

The stress of attending the funeral had brought on a headache. Thank goodness, there was no lunch to prepare back at the home, because everybody had gone on to the Guildhall to enjoy the lavish buffet provided by Mayfair Cuisine, the specialist caterers from Chichester. Mr Cavanagh had dropped him off at the front door, turned his car round, and made his way back to the Guildhall to stuff himself with goodies.

How he hated that lie, the lie he felt obliged to tell to preserve his own standing as a decent Englishman. *My grandfather was in the Free Polish Forces* . . . No one would ever know the truth.

Safe in his attic flat, Teddy had a shower, which helped relieve some of the nagging pain of his headache. He swallowed two co-codamols with a glass of water, and then opened his laptop. He'd been told not to gaze at a computer screen when he was suffering from a headache, but there were things that he wanted to read, and videos to watch of a kind that you wouldn't find on YouTube. Like many others who wanted to keep their internet history secret, he used the Tor browser. After half an hour, his head had cleared, and he threw himself gratefully on to his bed.

8. IN THE IRVING HOME'S CELLAR

It was while they were all milling around the forest of tomb-stones in the cemetery to reach the exit, that Gareth Pugh, the handyman at the Irving Home, approached DI French and DS Edwards, who had sat in the Lady Chapel during the funeral service.

'Inspector French!' cried Pugh, pointing to a man with a shock of thick white hair who was still standing near the graveside, talking to Terry Lucas. 'That's the man I heard threatening old Sir Frank five years ago. He hasn't changed a bit. The cheeky sod's turned up for his funeral!'

The man had seen Pugh pointing at him, and immediately tried to run away back towards the church. But he was going against the tide, and in moments the two detectives had caught up with him. He looked startled, and somewhat fearful. French recalled the letter Edwards had shown him earlier from the angry creditor. As he'd said to Edwards, 1948 was too long a time to hold onto a grudge over a debt — but this man was surely old enough to have been around back then.

'Mr John Brassington, I believe?' said French genially. 'You once sent a threatening letter to Sir Frank Taylor, and then, five years ago, you confronted him at his retirement

85

home, and made threats against him, which were heard by a witness.'

'Yes, I'm John Brassington,' said the man. 'But I'm not the John Brassington you're looking for. Or maybe I am, in part. Who are you, anyway? I've every right to come to Frank's funeral.'

The man had gone very pale, and begun twisting his hands together nervously.

'I'm Detective Inspector French of Oldshire CID, and this is Detective Sergeant Edwards. We're investigating the murder of Sir Frank Taylor. Can I ask what you meant when you said you're only John Brassington in part?'

'Well, Inspector French,' said Brassington, 'I admit that I tried to make myself scarce just now. I'm only down from Birmingham for the day, to see Chaim safely buried. There's quite a lot that I can tell you about Sir Frank Taylor, as he became. Are you going to arrest me?'

'Not yet, Mr Brassington, but we'd like to hear what you have to tell us about Sir Frank. Let us give you a lift to police headquarters, where we can take a statement from you. We're trying to amass as much background information as we can, you see, because often the cause of a crime is buried somewhere deep in the past. Like in 1948, for instance. It'll only take half an hour, and then you can be on your way.'

* * *

'They were bad times,' said John Brassington, later at the station. 'Nobody had anything. You stumbled to work in the morning over the debris of bombed-out buildings. That's what my father told me, anyway. Birmingham was very badly hit. And it was there, in the summer of 1945 — July or August, I'm not sure which — that my father, John Brassington senior, met Chaim Jakob Shapiro. It was my father who sent that letter to Shapiro, but it was me who had words with him five years ago at the old actors' home.

'My father was in the import–export business, and at the end of the war he secured a big contract to dispose of Army surplus equipment and stores. He did very nicely with that, and we never looked back. Dad came across Chaim Jakob Shapiro in a pawn shop at Perry Bar, where he was raising money on a few pieces of jewellery. Dad told me all this later, you understand. I wasn't even born, then.'

French felt a tide of embarrassment pass over him — he'd misjudged Brassington's age badly. 'And what did your father do, when he met Mr Shapiro?'

'He got into conversation with him, and learned that he was a Jewish refugee from Nazi Germany. He'd arrived in England with nothing but a few pounds that a British officer in Hamburg had given him, and his passport. Well, Dad was sorry for him, and made him a gift of two tons of Army-issue plum jam.'

'Two tins of jam?'

'No, Inspector, two *tons*.'

John Brassington laughed.

'Can you imagine it? Two tons of jam. Well, somehow, Chaim managed to set up a stall in one of the Birmingham markets, selling these big tins of jam for 1/9d. Within weeks he'd opened a little shop, and added other commodities to his stock, like soap powder, which was something else in short supply. He was doing very well. And then came the business of the loan.'

John Brassington frowned, and bit his lip.

'My dad was a shrewd businessman, and I'm running the business that he founded — me and my son Geoffrey. But Dad had a soft side to him, too, and it came to the fore where this Chaim Jakob Shapiro was concerned. He seemed fascinated by him. He was a German Jew, he told me, and yet he spoke perfect English. Anyway, Chaim came to see him one day, and asked for a loan of £500, to be repaid within six months. He said he wanted it to expand his little retail business. And so, like a fool, Dad lent it him. You'll appreciate, Mr French, that £500 was a small fortune in those days. You could buy a little terrace house for that. Well, the six months went by, and the loan wasn't repaid. Dad waited and waited, and was always put off with promises.'

French opened a filing cabinet and extracted a photocopied letter from a drawer.

'Here you are, Mr Brassington,' he said. 'Here's a copy of the letter your father wrote to Chaim Jakob Shapiro on 5 April 1948. You'll want to read what it says.'

Look here, Chaim, I won't wait much longer. I was very good to you, and helped you to set yourself up on your own. But you still owe me £500. If you don't pay this debt soon, cash or cheque, I'll send a couple of men round to rearrange your handsome features.

Brassington was evidently taken aback at the letter. 'Good grief, where did you get this from? That's Dad's writing, all right.' He looked back at the detectives. 'When I was old enough to understand, he told me about all this, and how he'd never been repaid. It rankled with him, you see, because one day Chaim Jakob Shapiro simply disappeared. He'd sold his shop, and moved on. We learned later that he'd joined a travelling repertory company under the name Frank Taylor, and from then onwards there was no looking back. I inherited my dad's resentment, because although I'm very comfortably off, I'm not a millionaire twice over, like Chaim, and his good fortune was founded on my dad's loan of £500.'

'Your father threatened Chaim Jakob Shapiro with violence—'

'It was just words. He was always threatening to rearrange people's features for them — including me, when he thought I was getting too uppity. But wait, there's something else written here: "Got Mr Friedlander to send him a solicitor's letter telling him to back off. I'll pay him when I'm able." The ungrateful sod. I didn't know about that letter.'

DI French glanced at DS Edwards and saw that he was relapsing into terminal boredom. There was nothing of significance in all this ancient history. John Brassington and his father could be written out of the investigation. There was just one remaining point that needed to be cleared up.

'Five years ago, Mr Brassington, you called on Sir Frank Taylor at the Irving Home for Retired Actors and were heard by a witness to threaten him. Apparently, you said he was as rich as Croesus, and that people in Birmingham were still waiting for their money. Then you allegedly threatened him unless he immediately paid his debts.'

John Brassington shifted uncomfortably in his chair. He broke out in a sweat and began to wring his hands in something approaching anguish.

'How did you find that out? Yes, that was five years ago, just after my father had died, still with the debt unpaid. It hit me badly, losing Dad. I don't think I was quite in my right mind when I came to see Chaim. Yes, I threatened him, but it was only words. I take after my father for that. Anyway, it did the trick.'

'What do you mean?'

'Well, there and then he took a cheque book from a drawer and wrote me a cheque for £500. And that was the end of the matter, after nearly seventy years. That's why I came to the funeral today — it was obviously too late to say sorry in case I'd frightened him but I wanted to show my face.' He shook his head. 'That cheque for £500 was worth a fraction of the sum that my father lent him all those years ago. He could have repaid that debt a lifetime ago, but chose not to. I guess we'll never know why.' He stood up then, looking impatient. 'Am I free to go, Inspector? I don't want to miss my train back to Birmingham.'

French couldn't be less inclined to let him go. He could feel in his bones that Brassington would have no scruples about murdering a frail old victim to get the message through to other potential defaulters. But he was reaching — you couldn't arrest a man just because you didn't like him. And if Brassington really had killed Sir Frank, he still had to figure out how he'd got past the locked doors and the CCTV.

* * *

'At any rate, sir,' sighed Glyn after Brassington had been escorted out of the interview room by a uniform, 'we can dismiss the whole Brassington saga from the investigation, and begin to look elsewhere.'

'Yes, but where, Glyn? What possible motive could any of those people at the Irving Home have for killing old Sir Frank?

'And all those documents SOCO and Noel Greenspan sent us don't advance this case one whit. There was his naturalization document, giving his original name as a German citizen, and his assumed name of Frank Taylor. Why Frank, I wonder? Perhaps he thought it sounded typically English. The passport, though, did tell us a grim story. Issued to Chaim Jakob Shapiro, it was stamped with the letter "J", following one of those Nazi edicts that continued the process of excluding the Jews from German society. Somehow, Chaim Jakob Shapiro managed to hang on to his passport through all those grim years. Perhaps he sewed it into his jacket. We don't know. But in the end it confirmed his identity when the war ended. Other Jewish refugees had nothing.'

DI French opened a drawer and brought out the photocopy of the passport's photograph page, which he handed to Glyn.

'Look at him,' he said, 'just a nice, pleasant boy, smartly dressed in his best jacket for the photograph. He was soon to be consigned to hell on earth but would later become one of Britain's most distinguished actors. These water stains . . . Maybe he washed his jacket, forgetting that the passport was sewn inside its lining. The bottom of the pages are virtually stuck together by a faded brown stain.'

'Sir,' said Glyn Edwards, 'has anything come back from Forensics about the passport? That brown stain may be blood.'

'Nothing yet — they had to send it off to a specialist because of the age of the document. You'd better chase them, though. We have samples of Sir Frank's DNA from the autopsy, and if that stain's blood, then we can confirm — or otherwise — that it's Chaim Jakob Shapiro's blood.'

DS Edwards had begun to examine the photograph through a powerful hand lens.

'He's got a scar under the right side of his chin,' he said. 'I wonder whether Dr Dunwoody saw it when he performed the autopsy?'

'Let's find out,' said DI French. 'I'll phone him now. He's at the mortuary all day today.'

Ten minutes later he put the phone down.

'Dunwoody saw no scar under Sir Frank's chin, and he can't spot any on the post-mortem photos, but he says it could have faded almost completely over the decades.'

'Still, sir, it's an interesting point that we could file away for the moment. Any progress on that tin box of letters? The ones in German?'

'I had them all translated by Dr Berg at the Oldshire University. They were from friends and relatives of Alphonse Shapiro, describing holidays, trips to Berlin and the Rhineland, and the latest gossip about who was going to marry who. They were all sent from various addresses in the Free City of Danzig to Herr Alphonse Shapiro at an address in Mannheim, in Baden-Wurttemberg.'

Glyn rose from his seat and stood at the window, looking out at the town hall. He was suddenly assailed by a conviction that the office was being peopled by phantoms, and that urgent voices were trying to tell him something. Everything that they had been examining had been shown to them by someone or something far deeper and far more intelligent than either of them. It was all wrong.

'How was he able to hang on to that passport?' he asked. 'Why was he allowed to keep it? The Nazis stole everything from the Jews. And anything they didn't want, they just destroyed. They just—'

For a moment the phantom voices returned, and he felt on the brink of a profound discovery, but then the voices receded, and there was nothing there but the banality of dead and faded documents, relevant now only to the dead man lying in the church graveyard.

'It's stuffy in here, Glyn,' said DI French. 'Open the window for a bit. I was almost persuaded that Sir Frank was indeed murdered by an outsider, but logic tells me that it must have been an inside job — nobody could have got into that building after ten o'clock without being recorded on CCTV, and that receptionist was too much of the noticing type to miss somebody like John Brassington sneaking in. Somebody at the Irving Home had it in for the old man, and all this delving into history is a mare's nest. We'll go back there, Glyn, and dig a bit deeper than we have. Somebody's laughing at us, and I intend to wipe the smile off their face.'

* * *

The day after the funeral, DS Edwards tried the handle of the cellar door, and found that it was locked. Someone had swept the little paved area free of cigarette butts, but the smell of cannabis still assailed his nostrils. He felt personally affronted at the uncompromising steel door that barred his entry to the cellars. There would be another way in through the house. Perhaps Trudy Vosper in reception would show him.

'As a matter of fact,' said Trudy with a little triumphant smile, 'there's no way into the cellars from inside the house. There used to be, years ago, but the door was bricked up. The house manager in those days thought it was better to have access only from the garden.'

'Could you give me a key to the outside door? I want to search those cellars, perhaps just to satisfy myself that there's nothing of interest there.'

'Of course. Please could you sign it out in this book, and return it to me personally when you've finished down there.'

'Thank you. Also — are you a smoker, by any chance?' asked Glyn. 'There were a lot of fag ends down there when I was here last, but they've gone now.'

'No, I don't smoke. We've four smokers on the staff: Cathy Billington, who smokes like a chimney, George Cavanagh, who ought to know better, and Teddy Balonek, the cook. He's forever sucking peppermints. Oh, and Terry Lucas. Anyhow, here's the key.'

The steel-clad door opened easily, and Glyn Edwards entered the cellars. There was a smell of lime-wash mingled with machine oil, and he could hear the quiet humming of the gas-fired central heating. The first room of the cellar contained two large professional petrol mowers, and an array of garden tools arranged in racks along the whitewashed walls. A narrow window in the far wall glowed green, suggesting that it was covered by ivy on the outside.

A doorway led into another cellar, this time dark and forbidding. A switch beside the door turned on two overhead light fittings, which flickered into life with a buzzing sound before they settled down. This cellar contained some old furniture, and a few card tables, their tops covered in torn green baize.

A third, smaller cellar revealed a work bench, complete with vice, and a cupboard in which various tools had been neatly arranged. The first two cellars had stone floors, but the third was covered in floorboards and, as Glyn made to leave, he trod on a loose board, and nearly stumbled. Bending down, he saw a section of the board had been sawn through. He felt around between the joists and found what felt like a cardboard box, which he gently slithered into view. It contained a couple of dozen neat little plastic bags, each sealed with tape. Plastic bags filled with white powder. Cocaine, maybe? If he was right, this amount could be worth a street value of thousands of pounds.

He stared at the stash for a moment, his mind working fast. Eventually, he got to his feet and carefully replaced the box. Best to leave things as they were for the moment until he'd talked with Inspector French. He left the cellars, locking the door behind him, and returned the key to Trudy in reception.

'Did you find anything?' she asked.

'Not much, really,' said Glyn. 'I'll be on my way now. Thanks for the help.'

As soon as he was out of earshot, he took out his mobile, eager to fill French in on his latest find. Then there was nothing for it but to wait for back-up.

It was a pleasant, sunny day, and he headed out to the grounds. He knew he needed to clear his throbbing head — his thoughts flicking compulsively between suspects and scenarios — before the team came wading in, and the gardens were mercifully deserted.

He suddenly thought of Sandra, and wondered whether she had got to her mother's safely. It would never have occurred to Sandra to phone him. He took his mobile from his pocket and called Sandra. No answer. Suddenly impatient, he phoned his mother-in-law's number in Southbourne.

'Why, Glyn, how nice to hear you. How are you? Is Sandra all right?'

'Sandra? Is she not with you?'

'No, she's not here. I thought she said she'd be here today, but you know what she's like. Very vague, is Sandra. Always was, even as a girl.'

'Well, she's not here. Where could she have gone?'

'Maybe she detoured to London to see that friend of hers, and then she'll catch the Bournemouth train tomorrow. She's done that before.'

Glyn Edwards felt a growing uneasiness. It wasn't so much not knowing where Sandra was, but not knowing who she might be with.

'I expect you're right,' he said. 'This friend — where does he or she live?'

'Ellen Chalmers. They were great pals when they were girls together here in Southbourne, before Ellen went to live in London. I've got her address somewhere. Just wait, Glyn, while I look it out.'

As he waited, Glyn mused that this wasn't the first time it had happened — a week's stay with Mum, but arriving two days late. Sandra's mother came back to the phone, and told him Ellen Chalmers' address in London. They exchanged a few civilities, and then Glyn rang off.

Banishing thoughts of Sandra from his mind, Glyn forced himself to focus on the matter at hand. Namely, Terry Lucas and his stash of class-A drugs. That lot he'd found down in the cellar would be enough to send Terry away for five years at least. But Terry Lucas was small fry. Who was his supplier? He thought suddenly of John Brassington, standing with the gardener at Sir Frank's graveside. They hadn't looked like strangers. In fact, now he thought about it, John Brassington had looked angry, threatening, even. The man was guilty of something, that was for sure.

9. HOOPER TAKES A HAND

The next morning, DI French and DS Edwards walked up the front drive to the Irving Home for Retired Actors. They had left late the night before after arresting Terry Lucas. He had confessed to storing the drugs in the cellar when confronted with the evidence, but he'd also been adamant that someone had given him away, and was willing to name names — now, at last, French had been able to contact Birmingham police about John Brassington, the kingpin, and his own force was searching for Colin Sagawa, Lucas's supplier. It had been a good day for the narcotics squad.

Now the lodge was virtually surrounded by police cars, and the building was cordoned off from the public by crime-scene tape. French's car was parked discreetly out of sight.

'I phoned Wickes yesterday afternoon. He said that his team found nothing much of significance in the lodge, except for a piece of paper giving Terry a list of possible contacts in the area, showing that he was indeed about to expand his drug-dealing operation. But there were other much larger hiding places in the cellars than the one you found. It was a big operation. God knows how many lives Terry Lucas and his cronies have ruined.'

'Did you tell Wickes that I'd been down there?'

'I did. You handled those bags of cocaine, so your fingerprints would have been all over them. I didn't want you to be arrested as an accomplice! He muttered something about "procedure", but agreed that you'd done the right thing. So that's that. Look, there's Dunwoody — I asked him to meet us here. He heard we were interested in Brassington and he said he had some old gossip that might be useful.

'Morning, Ray!' he called. 'Let's sit over here and you can tell us all about it.' They sat on a secluded bench half-hidden by tall evergreen hedges.

* * *

Hidden from sight was Anthony Hayling, sitting quietly on a rustic seat placed in front of a dilapidated potting shed. They could not see him, and he could not see them, but his hearing was particularly sharp for his age, and he could hear everything that they said.

* * *

'Brassington?' Dunwoody was saying. 'I'm sorry you had to let him go. He's a ruthless killer, you know. When I was attached to the Coventry Police, I was professionally involved in one of his vile murders. As always, we weren't able to pin the murder on him, but he did it, all right.'

'Who did he kill?' asked Glyn.

'The victim was a man called Michael Woodside, a business associate of Brassington's who decided to go straight, and posed an ever-present danger to Brassington. Woodside lived in a little Warwickshire village called Stanton St Luke, and we were called out there to find a blazing bonfire in the grounds of Woodside's house. In the middle of the bonfire, we found the half-incinerated remains of Michael Woodside. Apparently, he was a keen gardener, and had made and lit the bonfire himself. I made a preliminary examination of the remains, and found no soot deposits in the lungs, so he was dead when the fire started. I suppose that's a small mercy.'

'How were you able to examine the lungs?' asked French. 'Wouldn't you have to wait for the post-mortem to do that?'

'In my case of instruments I had things that made it fairly straightforward to look into the lungs. You don't really want me to go into the gory details, do you? That half-calcined mess that I saw in Woodside's garden was once a living human being. I always do what I have to do respectfully — and privately.

'I found when I performed the autopsy that Woodside had been shot in the back of the neck. The SOCOs went over the area with a fine-toothed comb, but didn't find an ejected cartridge. Maybe the killer picked it up before leaving the scene. The method of despatch suggested a gangland killing. Over at Coventry, we all knew that Brassington was behind it, but as always, we didn't find any concrete evidence to link him to it. One of his crooked mates was always there to provide him with an alibi.'

'What about the cremation, Ray? Do you think the blaze was meant as a warning to others? "Don't mess with the big guys."'

'It could be. But you know, it could also be partly an accident. After all, poor Woodside was a gardener, and he may have intended on starting the fire to burn up that pile of dead branches and other garden debris. Maybe he even brought the petrol cans to the scene himself. And you can imagine the rest. Brassington shoots him in the back of the neck, and he falls forward on to the pile of branches. Rather than pull him off, the killer douses the corpse in petrol, and sets the lot alight.' He sighed, shaking his head. 'Perhaps you're right, and it was a warning to others. If so, it seems to have worked. That man is unassailable.'

* * *

When Dunwoody left them, the two detectives went into the house, where they set up base in a little-used writing room.

'I think Dunwoody's right,' said DI French. 'Terry Lucas was getting too big for his boots, siphoning off the odd consignment of drugs for his own little enterprise, no doubt. I wonder whether Terry Lucas was at the funeral service?'

'Yes, he was, looking decidedly uncomfortable in a suit and tie — and I think you're right. Brassington was talking to him when Pugh pointed him out to us. But I lost sight of Terry when you and I went chasing after John Brassington.'

'And the outcome of that,' said DI French, 'was that we had to let him go. I've alerted the Birmingham police about Terry Lucas's confession. It's not enough for an arrest but they're keeping a close eye on John Brassington. That was a lame excuse he gave for being at the funeral — to apologize to Sir Frank for frightening him when he called for his money five years ago! Now that we know there's a link between Brassington and Terry Lucas, perhaps that can give us more insight into the murder of Frank Taylor.'

* * *

In the shelter of the space under a nearby staircase, Anthony Hayling was scribbling away in his diary. As he did so, he was formulating an outrageous plan. This John Brassington, the man who had frightened old Frank five years ago . . . All he needed now was to find out where Brassington lived, so that he could secure his telephone number. What were they saying now?

* * *

'They've done something about Brassington,' said DI French. 'They're going to put an unmarked car outside his house, and monitor his comings and goings. He's apparently a bona fide businessman, but he's got properties abroad, and a number of off-shore bank accounts. He's far wealthier than his legitimate business could have made him, but as yet they've no solid proof that he's into drug dealing.'

'And he really does live in Birmingham?'

'Oh yes. My contact was good enough to give me Brassington's address and telephone number.'

* * *

As he told them to his sergeant, Anthony Hayling gave a little sigh of satisfaction.

* * *

'That brown stain on Chaim Jakob Shapiro's passport,' said French, 'it was blood, but not Sir Frank's. Wrong DNA.'

The two detectives were back in DI French's office at Jubilee House.

'I'd almost forgotten about poor Sir Frank,' said Glyn Edwards. 'This business of Terry Lucas and the mysterious Brassington seems to have taken precedence for the moment.'

'I sent someone to make enquiries at the train station, but no one could remember a man with white hair waiting for any of the afternoon and early evening trains. But a beat constable saw a man of Brassington's description getting into a Rolls-Royce in that small car park near Cathedral Green.'

'I wonder how Noel Greenspan's getting on with his investigation? I heard from him the other day — that QC friend of his is going off to Europe to see if he can find anything relevant to Sir Frank's death in his early history. It sounds like a wild goose chase to me. But I'm not as sure as I was that the murder was an inside job. The fortress wasn't as impregnable as I thought. A drug-dealing operation had been going on there undisturbed under everyone's noses, and nobody noticed anything odd. Maybe we need to look further afield.'

'Do you really think that John Brassington's a killer, sir?'

'Yes, I do, and the police at Birmingham are inclined to agree. Anyway, they've got Brassington under surveillance twenty-four–seven. Perhaps we'll know more if he tries to make a move. All we can do is wait and see. Meanwhile, we seem to have stalled over the murder of Sir Frank Taylor. I think we'll have to ask Superintendent Philpot to call in Scotland Yard. Apparently, the chief constable's starting to get restless, and when he does that, the Lord Lieutenant always reacts in sympathy.'

Glyn Edwards made a movement of impatience.

'Sir, this business of John Brassington is preventing us from thinking straight. I still think Sir Frank's murder was an inside job. One of those actors, or maybe one of the staff, is hugging himself with glee.'

'You're right, Glyn. Let's go back to the Irving Home next week, and shake them all up a bit. We'll take a couple of uniforms with us for effect. We'll descend on them then. Somebody may panic, and give himself away.'

* * *

'Gentlemen, let me propose a toast.'

Charles Forshaw glanced along the table in the dining room, where the debris of Tony Hayling's birthday dinner had just been removed by Teddy Balonek the cook. It was just after nine, and Teddy had stayed late to clear away. He had blushed when Hayling had thanked him for his specially baked birthday cake, which had been covered in pink icing, with a blue '76' and the inscription: *Happy Birthday, Hooper of the Yard.* All the residents were there, lounging back at the table, drowsily appreciative of the special fare that Balonek had provided for them that evening. A lot of wine had been drunk, and one or two of them were eyeing the brandy decanter.

'Gentlemen,' said Charles, 'I know that you'll join with me in congratulating Tony on reaching the ripe old age of seventy-six, despite the various ravages of time that have slowed him down a bit of late. He suffers a lot, but I don't think any of us have ever heard him complain.'

There were murmurs of 'hear, hear', and a lot of banging on the table. They had reached the stage where everyone was happy to agree to anything that would prolong the festivities of the evening.

'It's been a melancholy time this last month,' Charles continued, 'with a murder on the premises, that of our dear old friend and fellow resident Frank Taylor. But, gentlemen, "the show must go on".' More murmurs and banging on the table. 'We were all of us in our time professional actors, so I need not remind you of what a distinguished career Tony had before he retired. He, and the characters he created on television were household names. So tonight, let us be thankful that this distinguished actor is one of our happy band. Gentlemen, I give you Anthony Hayling.'

The toast was drunk, and the glasses refilled. Everybody was determined to make a night of it. Charles looked at Anthony Hayling, who was occupying the place of honour at the head of the table. He seemed to be filled with new energy, and his eyes sparkled with mischief. When Charles had gone to fetch him from his room, he had quietly pocketed Charles's gold pen which had gone missing on the previous day. Tony would never entirely conquer his kleptomaniac tendencies. 'This is going to be a very special night, Forshaw,' he'd said. 'Sam Gossage and I have prepared a little surprise for you all.' Charles hoped that it would be nothing too inventive.

When Anthony Hayling rose to answer the toast, they saw him wince in pain, but he recovered quickly — his flinch a glimpse of the pain caused by his arthritis.

'Gentlemen,' he said, 'first, let me say that Charles Forshaw exaggerates the successes of my prime. That's because he's so modest. We all know that his acting had a sensitivity and refinement that I could never have attained. However, thank you for all the kindness you've shown me over the years. Thank you for putting up with my crustiness when things aren't going too well with me. And thank you for all the wonderful cards and presents!'

He suddenly looked grave, and Charles Forshaw saw tears gathering in his eyes.

'There's someone missing here tonight, gentlemen,' said Anthony Hayling. 'You know who I mean. I never seemed to have a good word to say about Frank when he was alive. I wish I'd been kinder to him, and more tolerant of his quirks and oddities. It was jealousy, you see. I was always jealous of him, and I hope that now he's in a better place, he'll forgive me. So may I now propose a toast: to the memory of Sir Frank Taylor.'

The toast was drunk in solemn silence. A buzz of conversation began, but Anthony Hayling had not finished.

'And now it's my turn,' he said, 'to entertain you all with a live drama. I don't need to remind you that the Irving Home has turned out to be a hotbed of crime — first murder and then drug running. It appears that our gardener, Terry Lucas, was a dyed-in-the-wool villain, operating a drug distribution business from the cellars here at the Irving Home. I'm very sorry about that. Terry and I were both "old lags" as the saying goes, and we got on well. But now for my little surprise. Tonight, gentlemen, I intend to force a murderer to confess.'

There was a shocked silence round the table.

'Steady on, Tony,' said Charles Forshaw eventually. 'I hope this isn't going to be your Agatha Christie moment! You're not suggesting that one of *us* murdered him?'

'No, no.' Anthony Hayling laughed. 'Ever since poor Frank was murdered I've maintained that none of us had anything to do with it. No, the murder victim I'm talking about was a man called Michael Woodside, and I believe his murderer is a man called John Brassington, who is currently holed up in his house in Birmingham, where the West Midland Police are waiting for him to make a move.'

'How on earth do you know all that?' asked Donald Mordaunt, the man who had quoted from *Macbeth* when Sir Frank Taylor's body had been discovered. 'Have you got some sort of connection with the police?'

Anthony Hayling laughed.

'Of course I have a connection with the police!' he cried. 'Am I not Hooper of the Yard? Well, it's Hooper who is going to make John Brassington hand himself over to the police!'

'Oh, steady on, Tony,' said Charles Forshaw. 'Let's not confuse fact with fiction.' To himself he thought: *He's had too much to drink, and he's going to make a fool of himself.* 'Let's call it a night.'

There was a landline telephone in the dining room, and at a nod from Hayling, Sam Gossage, the Cockney actor, brought it across to the table.

'All you've got to do, my friends,' said Hayling, 'is to be quiet, and listen.'

He opened his pocket diary, and dialled a number. They all sat in silence, hearing the dialling tone. Would anyone answer it? After a few tense moments, the handset was picked up at the other end of the line.

'John Brassington? This is Superintendent Hooper of Scotland Yard. The game's up, man. It's time for you to turn yourself in.'

Anthony Hayling's friends listened with growing awe. The elderly, arthritic man seemed to have grown in stature. His voice became strong and determined, with the arrogant tone of those in authority that had belonged to a bygone age. He was no longer Hayling, he was Hooper of the Yard. He sprang up from the table, apparently without pain, and they saw his face flush with anger. Anthony Hayling was giving the performance of his life.

'I tell you the game's up! Look out of the window. Do you see the police car parked in front of your house? What? *You were seen, man.* We have a witness who saw you shoot Michael Woodside dead. There was somebody on the other side of the hedge who saw you shoot him in the back of the neck. The Birmingham police knew that you possessed a .38 Smith and Wesson, and that's what you used to kill Woodside.'

Although they could not hear the words, they could hear a sort of high-pitched whine from the end of the line. John

Brassington was beginning to panic. 'Hooper of the Yard' continued his relentless interrogation. It was clear to everyone that Anthony Hayling had immersed himself completely in the role.

'Sergeant Pepper, fax that search warrant now to the West Midlands Police.'

'I'm on it, sir,' said Sam Gossage, executing a heavy walk away from the table.

'Now listen, Brassington,' the hectoring voice continued, 'you're going down for a long stretch, but I want to give you a fair chance. Our witness maintains that Michael Woodside fell forwards on to that bonfire, and that you only pulled his legs up on to it because you couldn't get him down on to the ground. Admit that, and the judge will take your admission into account.'

'Hooper' flushed with anger, and banged his fist down on the table.

'I tell you, Brassington, the game's up. Tomorrow, I will arrive in Birmingham with my team. If you give yourself up now, this evening, it will count in your favour. This is your last chance.'

They sat entranced, listening to the sobs at the end of the line before Hayling banged the receiver down. Under the relentless barracking of 'Hooper of the Yard', John Brassington had cracked. As Anthony Hayling made to sit down again at the table, his audience began to clap, and the delighted old actor responded with an involuntary bow.

* * *

'Last night,' said DI French, 'John Brassington walked out of his house and gave himself up to the police officers parked in the road outside. When he was taken to the police station, he made a formal written confession to the murder of Michael Woodside. He'll go down for life.'

'I thought Brassington was a weak-willed sort of man,' said Glyn, 'too anxious to be nice to us when we questioned him, but I never thought he'd give in so easily, just because there was a squad car parked outside his house.'

'It wasn't that, Glyn. Apparently, a superintendent from Scotland Yard phoned him up, and put the fear of God into him. Once he'd started his confession, he couldn't stop. He was a big player in the drugs game, with his son Geoffrey managing their supply lines in France and Spain. So, thankfully, the case of John Brassington is closed.'

* * *

It was only when the details of the case hit the papers the next morning that all hell was let loose. It started with the *Birmingham Post*, which mentioned that the West Midlands Police had been ably assisted by a Superintendent Hooper of Scotland Yard. The one o'clock news included an angry denial that Scotland Yard had been in any way involved in the John Brassington affair. There was no 'Superintendent Hooper' at the Yard. A letter in the *Daily Telegraph* asked whether the confession made by John Brassington was admissible, given that it had been partly obtained by fraud. However, various legal experts came forward to assure the public that Brassington's confession was entirely valid. As he had confessed to the murder of Michael Woodside, and the weapon used had been found in his house, he would appear before a judge for sentencing. It was certain that he would receive a minimum sentence of twenty-five years.

'*Hooper*?' said Glyn. 'That was Anthony Hayling's famous TV character. Do you think that it was Hayling—'

'I don't know, Glyn. It could have been Hayling. But then again it could have been anyone who seized on the name from having seen those repeats of the old shows on Talking Pictures. Do you want us to go out to the Irving Home and ask Hayling a few questions?'

'I think we should, sir. Maybe he had nothing to do with it, but if he did, it'll clear the air if he were to make a confession. The worse charge that could be brought against

106

him would be impersonating a police officer. But if it really was him, sir, part of me would want to congratulate him for bringing a ruthless killer to justice.'

'Anthony Hayling . . . You know what he did, don't you?' said French. 'At the height of his fame, he became involved with some high-class call girls who numbered a few MPs among their clientele. It was rather like the Profumo affair. Anyway, it did for Anthony Hayling. It was a reporter on the *Daily Express* who uncovered the whole squalid affair. That's when Anthony Hayling's career as an actor came to an abrupt end. Profumo was lucky. He was merely banished to the East End practically for life. Anthony Hayling served time in prison, for sharing drugs with some of those girls. When he was finally released, everybody had forgotten who he was. You could say that he paid dearly for his indiscretions.'

10. HAYLING GETS A CAUTION

The following Friday saw DI French and DS Edwards walking up the front drive to the Irving Home for Retired Actors.

As DI French rang the doorbell he said, 'That QC friend of Noel Greenspan's came to see me, and asked whether he could borrow Chaim Jakob Shapiro's passport to take with him on his European travels. I let him have it.'

'Scotland Yard may not like it, sir. It's a prime piece of evidence.'

'I know it is, Sergeant, but I've a lot of time for Lance Middleton. He's no amateur, and he has some very valuable connections in government circles. He's promised to bring it back.'

'I should hope so, sir! Just because—'

Edwards stopped as the door was opened by Trudy Vosper. She looked flushed with excitement.

'Have you come to arrest Anthony? Mary Helm's packing a suitcase for him, in case he has to go to jail. She's shedding buckets of tears, the silly girl.'

'As you have obviously guessed, Miss Vosper,' said French gravely, 'we have indeed come to talk to Mr Hayling, but there's no question of him going to jail. Not yet, at any rate. Would you please take us to Mr Hayling's room? The sooner we've interviewed him, the sooner we'll be on our way.'

If Anthony Hayling felt any fear of the two detectives, he certainly wasn't showing it. He looked about ten years younger. As soon as she saw them Mary Helm burst into tears.

'There, there, my dear,' said Hayling, 'don't take on so. We must all take our medicine when someone comes to dole it out to us. But you're a good girl, a true friend.'

He bent down and gave her a kiss on the cheek. She began to sob, and rushed from the room, dragging the suit-case behind her.

'So, officers,' said Anthony Hayling, 'this is the moment of reckoning. Please sit down. And ask me anything you like.'

'Well, Mr Hayling,' said DI French, 'would I be right in assuming that it was you who phoned John Brassington, purporting to be a police officer? And if so, how on earth did you know what to say?'

'First, Inspector, let me plead guilty to ringing up that villain, and making him confess. But I didn't really imper-sonate a police officer, did I? I merely reprised my role as Hooper of the Yard. It was a prank, Inspector, and it cer-tainly got results! As to how I knew what to say, well, I was always good at loitering in the wings, and happened to be present, but unseen, when you and Sergeant Edwards there imagined that you were not being overheard.'

'You mean—'

'I mean that I heard everything that you said in the vege-table garden, and later in the writing room, and then I strung it all together as a kind of script, the kind of thing Hooper of the Yard used to have. John Brassington was an involuntary member of the cast.'

Despite himself, French burst into laughter.

'Really, Mr Hayling,' he said, 'what an incredible, mad thing to do! Whatever possessed you to jeopardize your lib-erty in that way? I gather that it was your birthday? Perhaps you had had too much to drink?'

'Maybe I had, Inspector. Yes, now I think about it, you're probably right. But it was marvellous, you know! All the fellows clapped and cheered when I'd finished. Now, what are you going to do to me? Poor Mary's already packed a case to accompany me to Dartmoor.'

'I'm going to issue you with a police caution, Mr Hayling, and that will be the end of the matter. Don't ever do that kind of thing again — it is against the law. That's the end of the caution. Now, let me congratulate you on bringing a very evil man so swiftly to justice!'

'Thank you, Inspector. Little Mary will be much relieved. But seriously, I do recognize that it was an irregular and reckless thing to do, and there won't be any kind of repetition.'

Anthony Hayling looked grave for a moment. He shifted in his chair, wincing with pain as he did so.

'I take it that you know all about me, Inspector, and you, Sergeant? I'm referring to my past. Yes, I see you do. I served time in prison. Terry Lucas did two stretches at Lea Hill. I held no brief for Terry's crimes, but he and I shared a bond. We were both old lags, and knew each other's measure — he was never a crime kingpin, always the fall guy. It wasn't just vanity or bravado that made me put on that show the other night. I heard you saying that John Brassington was potentially Terry's supplier and I wanted to make sure that the man behind his crimes was brought to justice and to prison. Let the kingpin do the time, for a change.'

It was, thought French, a speech well delivered, but it was obviously sincere.

'We'll be on our way now, Mr Hayling,' he said.

'You've still no idea who murdered poor old Frank, I suppose? No, I thought not. Maybe it'll always remain a mystery. Well, now that I'm free from the threat of prison, I can turn my thoughts to my new career.'

'Why, sir, what do you mean by that?'

'I mean journalism. The story of my successful ruse has made the national papers, and one of the bigger red-tops has offered me a tidy sum to tell my life story, which I'll be only too happy to do. It's a pity *The News of the World* isn't around these days — they'd have loved it. Especially the scandal.'

'Won't that be — er — rather difficult to recount?'

'Well, yes, but people these days seem to have quite the appetite for it. The newspaper assured me that all would be well, and that my story would be specially written for me by a ghost writer who is skilled in presenting villains as misunderstood goodies.'

'Well, sir, congratulations! I hope it all goes well with you.'

* * *

'Inspector French!'

It was the sharp-eyed, handyman, Gareth Pugh, who beckoned the two policemen to follow him into the service yard behind the kitchens, where he had been busy tipping the contents of various bins into two tall middens.

'It may be nothing, sir,' said Pugh, 'but when I was emptying rubbish from the house, I came across these two newspapers. They're German, as far as I can tell, and as Sir Frank was murdered with a German dagger, I thought you'd want to have a look at them.' He handed them the two papers, and went back into the house through the kitchen door.

'I know this one,' said French. 'It's the *Frankfurter Allgemeine Zeitung,* a popular German daily. It's dated last week — last Wednesday. But this other one, *Der Danziger Vorposten*, is dated 7 June 1941. What we now call Gdansk, in Poland, was still called by its German name Danzig during the war. This is a Nazi paper — look, there's a photograph of Hitler visiting one of the shipyards.'

'Do you read German, sir?'

'I don't, no. So, somebody here at the Irving Home likes to see a German paper from time to time, and is suddenly anxious to throw away a pre-war Nazi newspaper that he must have kept as a souvenir for years. We'll keep that under lock and key back at the office. Meanwhile, we've done our duty here, and given Mr Hayling his caution. Let's get back to Jubilee House.'

* * *

'Any chance of a cuppa, Teddy?'

Liz Bold came into the kitchen carrying a mop and bucket.

Teddy Balonek, who was putting the finishing touches to a very large shepherd's pie, checked the temperature on one of his ovens, and then switched on the electric kettle. It was just after eleven o'clock, and a cup of tea would be welcome.

'You look a bit hot and bothered today, Liz,' said Teddy. 'What have you been up to?'

'I've been blitzing poor old Sir Frank's room. All the furniture's been put in store, except for the items that belong to the home, and Gareth Pugh pulled up the fitted carpet and stored it in that room behind the garages. I've been scrubbing the floorboards with plenty of hot water and disinfectant. Oh, thanks, Teddy, that's lovely.'

Liz sat down at the kitchen table, and cradled the mug of tea in her hands after the morning's hard work.

'Mr Cavanagh said that they're phasing out carpets in the guests' rooms in favour of laminate,' said Teddy. 'Something to do with health and safety, apparently.'

'It's funny,' said Liz Bold, 'there's no trace of Sir Frank in room 2, now. It's as though he was never even here.'

'He'll always be here,' said Teddy Balonek, heavily. 'They can't leave the scene of their death, you know — earth-bound spirits, they call them.'

Liz sighed.

'I thought you liked him.'

'Whether I liked the man or not, I tell you he's still here. He's neither in heaven, hell, or purgatory. I'll make us a couple of rounds of toast.'

Liz watched him as he busied himself at the grill. She knew that he was thirty-five, and although he was a good-looking man, he wasn't married. He was very friendly and kind, but he'd never talk about his background, never mentioned his parents. He'd occasionally speak about his grandfather, who'd served in the Free Polish Air Force, but even then, he'd turn the conversation to other channels. Bit of a mystery man.

The door opened, and Tracey Potter came into the kitchen. Teddy and Liz briefly acknowledged her, and continued their conversation. Tracey sat on a stool at the far side of the kitchen, and began to peel potatoes.

'But I think you must be right about Sir Frank still being here,' said Liz, when she'd eaten her round of buttered toast.

'What do you mean?'

'Well, when I went into room 2 at nine yesterday, there was only a lot of screwed-up brown paper in the waste paper basket. I suddenly realized that I'd forgotten to bring the Cif from my cupboard, and when I came back with it, there were two newspapers in the basket, as well! Foreign, they were, by the looks of them. Gareth came in, then, and took the basket away for me. Some people said that Sir Frank was actually a German; maybe they were right, and it was his ghost that threw those papers away.'

She laughed in disbelief at her own silly fancy. Teddy glanced at the kitchen clock.

'Time I put this shepherd's pie in the oven,' he said. 'Never mind the dead, Liz. It's our job at the moment to look after the living!'

* * *

Tracey Potter had finished her morning's stint at the Irving Home, and taken the bus into Oldminster town centre, where she met her friend Shona for coffee. Shona was still at school, in her final year at the comprehensive. She was thrilled to know that Tracey was once more involved in a gruesome murder.

'Anyway,' said Tracey, 'that's what he said, and she believed him. But I saw what really happened, and it wasn't that at all.'

'Maybe it's a clue,' said Shona, sipping her coffee. 'Maybe you should go and see that nice man who bought us a sandwich. Detective Sergeant Edwards.'

'My dad would murder me if I got mixed up with the police again,' said Tracey. 'But it's not my fault. People don't seem to think I count as a real person. "Oh, it's only Tracey", they say. But I'm not as daft as I look.'

'No,' said Shona.

'Maybe I will tell that Mr Edwards, but not yet. I like it at the Irving Home, but you've got to watch yourself with all them actors about. Mr Hayling gave me a twenty-pound note the other day, and told me to buy him twenty Lambert and Butler. He said to keep the change.'

'Oh, no, Tracey, don't!'

'Oh, I didn't. I brought him the change, and he wouldn't have it.' She remained thoughtful for a while, and then said: 'But it wasn't like that. I saw what I saw. So maybe I'll tell Mr Edwards after all.'

* * *

'Well, well,' said George Cavanagh, 'I can't believe it!'

'Believe what, George?' asked Gladys Trickett.

'This is a letter from our solicitors. Sir Frank Taylor left the home £50,000 in his will! I thought he'd leave us something, but not such a big sum as that.'

'It's wonderful news, George, it shows how much he appreciated this place, and all that we tried to do for him. Oh dear! How kind!'

Gladys's eyes filled with tears, which she quickly wiped away with a tissue from the box on George Cavanagh's desk. She wasn't one for making a fuss, however sincerely she felt things.

'It means we can start work on that nursing suite,' said Cavanagh. 'We could name it after him. We both want standby nursing facilities here at the Irving Home, and Sir Frank's bequest will make that a real possibility.'

'Did they give you any more details about his will?'

'Yes. He left two million pounds, free of estate duty. Fancy making money like that, just by pretending you're other people! The bulk of his estate goes to various charities, including one in Germany — an old soldiers' association. Oh! I didn't see that. He's left a thousand pounds to each of the residents! What a kind thought! That'll go down well with our old actors. He's also left "a very large sum" — it doesn't say what — to found a drama school for British and Commonwealth students. Well, God bless him. I'm glad we were able to make his final years as happy as we could.'

Gladys Trickett seemed to be far away and George asked her what was wrong.

'I'm thinking of Cathy Billington,' she said. 'You and I can't go on much longer without a PA.'

'I know, I know. But I've had a doctor's note to say she's having a bad bout of flu, and not a hint of when she'll be back. You'll agree that she's outstandingly good at her job, and we're somewhat lost without her — she knows our guests so well, and has become an essential part of the Irving Home. So, what ideas do you have? Incidentally, I think you should assume the official title of matron, Gladys, because that's who you really are.'

* * *

Sandra's friend Ellen Chalmers lived in a terraced house in a pleasant, tree-lined street in Fulham. DI French had given Glyn a couple of days' leave without asking for a reason, and he had come to London in order to find out what Sandra had been doing during the time that she had not been with her mother. It was comforting to know that she was now safe at Southbourne — he'd called Sandra on Sunday afternoon, and spoken with her briefly without letting her know that he was using his professional skills to find out what she was up to.

'Yes, she stayed with me for two days before catching the train to Southbourne. Is anything the matter, Glyn?'

'I'm just curious to know what she's been up to, Ellen. I suppose I'm jealous. She never tells me anything, these days.'

He knew that Ellen Chalmers was a shrewd woman, and a successful theatrical producer in the West End. If he played his cards wrong, she would clam up about what her friend was doing. To present himself as an archetypal jealous husband would probably do the trick.

'There's no need to be jealous, Glyn,' said Ellen. 'You should know better than that.'

'Then why does she come to London without telling me? What does she do when she comes here? What—'

'Sit down, Glyn. You've been prowling round the room like a caged tiger since you came. Just sit down, and listen to what I've got to say. She comes to London to see a doctor, a specialist at the Royal London Hospital. Her own doctor in Oldminster recommended him.'

'A doctor? Why, what's the matter with her? She never told me she was ill.'

Ellen gave him a rather unnervingly appraising look.

'She thought you'd despise her. She said to me: "I can't tell Glyn. He already sees me as a failure for giving up my job, so I can't talk to him about this."'

'But what is this illness?' Glyn tried and failed to keep the panic from his voice.

'Oh, she's ill, right enough, and I suppose I'll have to break her confidence and tell you what it is. It's her mind, not her body, that's the cause for concern. The doctor she's seeing is a behavioural psychologist.'

Mental health problems . . . Why hadn't she told him? *Despise* her? How could she have thought that?

'What should I do, Ellen? I see now that I've been too concerned with my own trivial wants, too absorbed with my work . . . Poor girl! What should I do?' he repeated.

'Well, if I were you, Glyn,' said Ellen, 'I'd ask her to tell you the whole story. Believe me, once she sees that you're showing some *concern* for her instead of criticism, there'll be no stopping her. She's told me a lot, but I'm not going to repeat it third-hand. Go home, Glyn, and ask her to tell you about Dr Alexander Sarner, and what he's doing to bring her back from the brink.'

Glyn stood up. It was time to go. Before he could reach the door, Ellen spoke again.

'Glyn,' she said, 'I'm going to tell you some of the things that Sandra told me as a friend, things that I think you should hear about now. Sandra told me that you were too good for her, that you were a famous detective, and that if she didn't "get her act together" as she put it, she would lose you. She said . . . She said that she should never have married you, because she knew that you only married her because you felt sorry for her—'

'That's absolute rubbish! I married her because I loved her.'

'I know; but Sandra doesn't. It's time for you two to listen to each other. As far as I can understand it all, you are part of her problem, and she's part of yours. Go and talk to her, now.'

11. THE TRUTH ABOUT SANDRA

Glyn and Sandra sat together on the couch in their living room. Stepladders and rolls of wallpaper formed part of the background, but neither of them saw these things: they saw only each other.

'How long have you been seeing this Dr Sarner?' he asked.

'Two years.'

'*Two years?*'

'Yes. I didn't want you to know. I thought you'd despise me, and I was terrified of losing you. *Terrified* . . . I'd arrange to visit Mum, and then spend a couple of days in London, seeing Dr Sarner. Only Ellen knew what I was doing. Mum had no idea.'

'You could have confided in me, love. I'd have done anything to see you well again. Tell me about this Dr Sarner.'

'He's a psychotherapist, using special techniques to treat anxiety disorders, depression, and mental illness. It didn't take him long to get to what he called the "trigger", the incident that set me off into this spiral of mental decline.'

'And what was this trigger?'

'Oh, Glyn, it was the fact that I could no longer have any children after that miscarriage.'

Sandra began to cry quietly, and Glyn hugged her close.

'I'd let you down, Glyn, I wasn't fit to be your wife. That's how I felt. And that led to the next stage of this illness.'

'The next stage?'

'I felt worthless, Glyn, and Dr Sarner said that I then began to adapt my behaviour to echo that worthlessness. So I began to neglect the house, because that was what a worthless wife would do. Dr Sarner called it "a carapace of neglect". I had created it myself, Glyn, and to make matters worse, there was always the example of DI French's wonderful, perfect wife, Moira, to reproach me, the wife who gave him a baby.'

Sandra began to cry again. Glyn said, 'Are these sessions with Dr Sarner doing you any good?'

'Oh, yes, they are. He's made me confront my own demons, and not very long from now he'll banish them entirely. But all this deceit is holding me up. I'm terrified that you'll stop me visiting Mum, which would mean the end of my visits to Dr Sarner.'

'Did you really think that I'd stop you from visiting your mother?' asked Glyn incredulously. 'Now listen, Sandra. I'm one hundred per cent behind this therapy. No need for deceit any longer. No doubt Dr Sarner could fix up regular sessions, and maybe I could come with you occasionally, and take you out to lunch somewhere afterwards.'

Sandra stood up, her eyes sparkling. As she stood there, she looked to Glyn like a new woman.

'Oh, Glyn,' she cried, 'this is going to be a new beginning for us! The three of us working together will very soon bring me back to myself, I'm sure of that.'

She suddenly blushed, and sat down again. She held Glyn's hand, and he waited to see what final revelation she was going to make.

'We're both thirty-eight,' she said.

'Yes.'

'Well, Dr Sarner wondered whether we'd ever considered adopting a child? I mean, a *baby*, Glyn.'

'A baby?' Glyn began to feel dizzy at the mere possibility of such a thing. 'Well, Sandra, I heartily agree. Mrs and Mrs

Edwards — and possible baby — have a bright future ahead of them!'

* * *

'We need to probe deeper.'

DI French stared gloomily at the screen in front of him, sighing at the sight of an email he'd received that morning. It was a formal notification from Scotland Yard, telling him that if help was required in solving the murder of Sir Frank Taylor, then a formal request from his superintendent would result in Detective Chief Superintendent Airey being placed at their disposal.

'Superintendent Philpot doesn't like the idea, Glyn,' he said. 'He thinks we ought to be able to solve this crime ourselves. I think he's right, but if the chief constable starts to put on the pressure, then he'll have to give in. We need to go back to the Irving Home and ask some more questions. One of them did it, Glyn.'

'Yes, sir, but *why*? We've discreetly checked up on the nursing staff, and they're all who they say they are. So is Liz Bold, and that handyman — what was his name? Gareth Pugh. George Cavanagh's a leading light in the community, and has been for years. Cathy Billington, too, for that matter. Teddy Balonek—'

'Yes, our Teddy,' DI French interrupted. 'Do we know where he lives?'

'Yes, he's got a sort of self-contained flat in the attic storey. Why, sir, what are you thinking?'

'I'm thinking that he'd have been ideally placed to creep down in the early hours of the morning, murder Sir Frank, and slip back upstairs again. What else do we know about him?'

'His granddad was Polish.'

'How do we know that?'

'Because he told us!'

'Exactly. What else do we know about this grandfather?'

'He served in the Free Polish Forces during the war. I think it was in the air force.'

'And how do we know *that*?'

'Because he told us!'

'Yes. So I think we should dig a bit deeper into Teddy Balonek's history, and a good place to start would be the Polish Centre in Archway Road. Maybe they could tell us something about Balonek.'

'You're fishing, sir.'

'Yes, Glyn, I know. But I think it's worth doing. We'll know much more about this whole business when Lance Middleton gets back from Germany, but that doesn't mean that we should sit here idly in the meantime. What time is it now?' He glanced at his watch. 'Three. Go down to Archway Road, Glyn, and see what the Polish community have to say about Teddy.'

When Glyn Edwards had gone, DI French thought to himself: Something's happened to Glyn. He's looking more relaxed and cheerful than he's been for months. *What did he get up to on those two days' leave?*

* * *

When DS Edwards stepped out into Jubilee Drive, he saw Tracey Potter standing by the railings surrounding the police car park. Her face brightened when she saw him, and she ran across the road to speak to him.

'I've been waiting for you to come out, Detective,' she said. 'It's about them foreign newspapers. Liz thought that Sir Frank's ghost had put them in the wastepaper basket, but that wasn't true. Teddy pretended not to know anything about it, but that wasn't true, because it was Teddy who put those papers in the basket. I saw him do it, though he didn't see me. I thought you should know. Do you think it's a clue?'

'Thanks for telling me, Tracey, that's really helpful. If ever you have any other clues to tell me about, don't go waiting outside like that. You come into Jubilee House, and ask for me by name at the desk. Then they'll send you straight up to my office.'

He watched the girl walk away in the direction of the high street, and then hurried back to his office, where he retrieved the two German newspapers from a locked drawer. He had no knowledge of German, but maybe someone at the Polish Centre did.

* * *

The Polish Centre occupied two shops in Archway Road, a busy thoroughfare to the south of the train station. Business appeared to be brisk. A number of people were engaged in filling out various forms, supervised by an elderly man in a baggy suit. Others were playing pool, while a third group could be seen watching a football match on Sky Sports in a back room. There were posters on the walls, presumably giving advice in what Glyn regarded as Europe's most impenetrable language.

The elderly man looked up as he entered. His face was creased, but the creases looked as though they were the result of a lot of smiling.

'Can I help you, sir?' he asked.

'I hope so,' said DS Edwards. 'I'm seeking information about a man living here in Oldminster with links to the Polish community, or so we believe. His name's Teddy Balonek, and he works as cook in the Irving Home for Retired Actors. My name's Detective Sergeant Edwards.' He showed the man his warrant card.

'Pleased to meet you, Sergeant Edwards. I'm the manager here. My name's Jan Milczarek. Come upstairs and have a cup of tea with me.'

They mounted a bare wooden staircase, and entered a room overlooking the street. It was a combination of office and reference library, with a sink unit and draining-board by the window. Milczarek switched on the kettle, and soon they were both enjoying a mug of tea.

'There are over sixty Poles working in Oldminster and the surrounding villages,' said the manager. 'This place can offer all sorts of advice to newly arrived workers — how to fill in application forms for grants, how to join English classes, that kind of thing. It's also a relief for some of the younger ones to be able to speak their native language for half an hour. So tell me this Polish man's name again.'

'His name's Teddy Balonek. But he's English, really — his grandfather was Polish.'

'Ah, yes. Tadeusz Balonek. I know of him, Sergeant, and I've met him once or twice at Polish "do's" organized by St Theresa's Church. Although he was born in England, I know he thinks of himself as Polish rather than British.'

'So he speaks the language?'

Jan laughed.

'Oh, yes, I've heard him speaking Polish. Most people who came to England in the war ensured that their language didn't die out — his grandfather seems to be no different.'

'You don't think he could be a German?'

Jan frowned. 'Sergeant, what are you trying to prove here?'

'We are trying to solve the mystery of Sir Frank Taylor's death. We've made little progress so far, so I'm compiling dossiers on all the staff working at the Irving Home. We're convinced that the murderer is someone actually living at the Irving Home.'

'And why do you think that Teddy Balonek is German?'

'Because I think he reads German newspapers, and then disposes of them when he thinks nobody's watching him.' Glyn handed the two papers to the manager.

'Yes, well of course, many Poles can read German, so there's no reason why Teddy shouldn't, if there's something there that interests him. This is the Frankfurt daily paper, widely read in Germany. And this — oh, this is something more sinister, Sergeant. This other paper is a copy of *Der Danziger Vorposten*, dated 7 June 1941. I can tell you a lot about this. It was a Nazi paper, published during the occupation of Poland. I wonder why Teddy has it?'

He cleared the mugs from the table, and spread the broadsheet paper out. Glyn watched him as he began to read it silently, his face grim with concentration.

'Yes, yes . . . Plenty of articles on Germany's triumphs in the East, and its success in making its conquered territories Jew-free. Here are lists of appointments in the government and civil service. And here — ah! *News from the General Government*. That was what the Germans called the greater part of Poland. *Appointments in the Polish Criminal Police*. This is a list of new members of that particular force made in June 1941. Let's see . . . There!' He stabbed the paper with his finger. '*Mateusz Balonek*. That could be Teddy Balonek's relative. You could check up on that by contacting the Polish Embassy.'

'Teddy told us that his grandfather fought in the Free Polish Forces.'

'Maybe he did — there are plenty of Baloneks in Poland — but why does Teddy have this particular paper if it hadn't some kind of sentimental value? Where did you find it?'

'Balonek disposed of it in a wastepaper basket when he thought that nobody could see him.'

'Hmm . . . I won't try to teach you your job, Sergeant, but I suggest you check that the story of his grandfather serving in the Free Polish Forces is true. Again, the embassy will be able to help you with that.'

The manager closed the paper and sat back in his chair. He looked distressed and almost tearful.

'I am a historian of modern Poland,' he said, 'and I can tell you all you need to know about the Polish Criminal Police. The force was established by the German occupiers in 1940, and it lasted until 1945. It was a genuine detective police force, and its members, who were armed and wore civilian clothing, were part of the auxiliary police.'

'What kind of people joined this special force?'

'The SD Commander in the General Government issued a decree calling upon all pre-war criminal police officers to report for duty on pain of severe punishment. Most of these officers obeyed, and the force was duly constituted. Although

operating as a civilian police force, it was ultimately controlled by the SS and the SD.'

'But they were real police?'

'Yes, they were, and it looks as though Teddy Balonek's
grandfather was one of them — if, of course, he's the "right"
Balonek. They were trained at the Security Police School of
the Reichsfuhrer SS and at other places. And they were very
successful in doing their job.'

'Did many Poles join the Criminal Police?'

'Yes. At the beginning of 1945 there were over two and
a half thousand officers.'

'Dare one ask what their duties were?'

'They dealt with robberies, assaults, murders and sab-
otage. Special units looked into small thefts and burglary,
moral crimes, such as rape, and the registration of wanted
persons. They were trained in forensic techniques and had a
very up-to-date photographic crime laboratory.'

'Well, it all sounds very orthodox.'

'Yes . . . but the officers were also trained in the business
of searching for Jews in hiding. Many of those men became
fanatical supporters of the Nazis, and although we Poles were
supposed to be of an "inferior" race, the Germans had a high
regard for the Polish Criminal Police.'

As he walked back to his car, Edwards thought about
Teddy Balonek . . . Was all this talk of wartime police units
to be another mare's nest? It would do no harm to check
with the Polish Embassy. Superintendent Philpot was already
down in London on business. It'd be no problem for him to
make an extra stop at the embassy to make some enquiries.

12. THE BERLIN ARCHIVES

Lance Middleton relaxed in his seat, closed his eyes, and listened to the quiet throbbing of the jet engines. He liked Lufthansa. The staff were efficient and courteous, and the cabin crew treated you like real people. They had left Heathrow at noon, and they would put down at Munich International to collect more passengers before continuing to Berlin's Tegel Airport.

His work with a group of advocates attached to the European Court of Human Rights had finished far earlier than he had expected, and he had returned to London to deliver a brief report to the Foreign Office before setting out on his mission to delve into the early life of the man who had ended up as Sir Frank Taylor, but who had started it as Chaim Jakob Shapiro.

He relished these commissions from Noel Greenspan and Chloe McArthur. They were not humdrum affairs: there was always an element of the *recherché* about them. Their last foray had taken them into the interesting cellars of an abandoned lunatic asylum. Now, he was to worm his way into the good graces of a German Benedictine prior, in order to make him divulge whatever dark secrets he knew about a certain Brother Anselm, who signed himself with the initials KH.

Chaim Jakob Shapiro . . . Did Noel Greenspan know that the name 'Shapiro' meant that your family originated in the German city of Speyer? Probably. It was sometimes disconcerting, the things that Noel knew. He had given Lance the photograph album, and photocopies of all the documents that had been stored in the box that Sir Frank Taylor had entrusted to Charles Forshaw. On his own initiative, Lance had procured Chaim Jakob Shapiro's passport from DI French, his request being boosted by a letter from his friend Peter Hamilton at the Foreign Office. French had told him that in the passport photograph they had detected a scar under Shapiro's chin, though Dr Dunwoody had not seen anything like that during the autopsy.

Lance Middleton took a taxi from the airport to the Adlon Hotel, in Unter den Linden, within sight of the Brandenburg Gate. A firm believer in looking after the inner man, he was familiar with all three restaurants and the two splendid bars, where his request for some obscure vintage was invariably met with a smile of recognition. He would dine at six, and then go out to the Konzerthaus in Gendarmenmarkt, where there was to be a concert of some of Schumann's piano works. And in the morning, he would call upon his friend Heinz Liebermann, who was a senior officer in the BKA, the Federal Criminal Police Office. He was almost certain that Liebermann would be able to reveal some of the secrets of Chaim Jakob Shapiro's bloodstained passport.

* * *

Heinz Liebermann's office was in a quiet street in the pleasant suburb of Wilmersdorf. It occupied the whole first floor of a restored pre-Second World War building. There were no signs at the door to say who occupied the premises, though a uniformed concierge would admit only those visitors who had an appointment. Lance Middleton was one of them.

Heinz greeted him with a smile and a handshake. 'So you're staying at the Adlon? Well, Lance, you always liked your creature comforts, even when we were schoolboys.' He chuckled before clapping his hands together. 'Now, you want me to look at an old passport?'

Lance handed him Chaim Jakob Shapiro's passport, and watched his friend as he examined it through a hand lens. Liebermann was a slight, gaunt man, with thinning sandy hair. He wore a dark suit, and a white open-necked shirt. Lance heard him suppress a sigh as he put the passport down on the table in front of him. *Memories*, thought Lance. *Would Germany ever be free from its Nazi past?*

'You see there the "J" over-stamp, Lance? It stood for *Jude* – Jewish. Can you imagine the shame most decent modern Germans feel when they see things like that? I can find out for you when this passport was issued — at the moment, all the written details have faded away. What age would he have been here? Fourteen?

'This Sir Frank Taylor — was this his passport? How did it come to be stained in this way? I have seen many like this, Lance, damaged by water, and sometimes stained with blood, but they were taken from abandoned rooms in deserted concentration camps and other hellish places set up by the Nazi regime. Sometimes they were found sewn into the lining of garments, found when the corpses were being prepared for burial or cremation after the war. Your Sir Frank was fortunate — he was able to hang on to his passport, and no doubt it served as a key to opening various doors in post-war Germany as he made his way through the turmoil to his destination in England.'

'Fortunate indeed,' said Lance. 'Something for which we can all be thankful.' Lance handed Heinz the small photo album.

'This is interesting,' said Heinz. 'A little family group posing in their garden.'

'We thought that the boy in those pictures could have been Chaim Jakob Shapiro, but then we saw the swastika necklace worn by the mother.'

'Yes, they look like a typical bourgeois family, the pictures taken with a box camera. And here's a picture of Hitler with Goering and Goebbels. That building they're standing in front of was called the House of the Physicians.'

Liebermann idly turned the pages of the album, and then suddenly sat up straight in his chair.

'Look at this!' he cried. 'Something that the boy in the photographs has written. "Our house in Kaiser Wilhelm Strasse, Leipzig. Me with Mummy and Daddy. May,1934. This book belongs to Franz Schneider, aged 10. Heil Hitler!" *And it's written in English!* I know who these people were.' Heinz stood up suddenly. 'Excuse me, I must go downstairs to the archive. I'll be back as soon as I can.'

He all but bolted from the room, and Lance could hear him clattering down the stairs to the ground floor. He returned in half an hour, clutching a dusty and faded brown folder, which he placed on the table.

'This file tells us all we need to know about the Schneiders,' he said. '"Mummy and Daddy" were Rudolf and Helga Schneider, who were both English teachers at different schools in Leipzig. They had both studied at London University, and later at Heidelberg. They were renowned locally for their outstanding skills in English, and as you can see from that inscription in the album, they brought up their son Franz to be virtually bilingual.'

'Well,' said Lance, 'they seem to have been very worthy people, so what was the snag?'

'The snag, Lance, was that they were all fanatical Nazis — the boy as well. The parents were early party members, and they brought up their son to follow in their footsteps. "Very worthy", perhaps, from a Nazi point of view, but not from ours.'

Lieberman opened the file and took out a typed sheet.

'On various dates between September 1939 and May 1942, they denounced seventeen neighbours and two relatives to the Gestapo. When the two relatives were shot as traitors, the Schneiders held a party for the local children.'

'Good God! What happened to the seventeen neighbours?'

'Seven were found to be innocent. Eight served terms of imprisonment. Two of them were murdered in Dachau. Oh, and when the two relatives were shot, Heinrich Himmler sent the Schneiders a personal letter of thanks for their loyalty to the Führer and the party. His letter's here, in this file: "It is on the foundation of patriots like you," he wrote, "that the future of National Socialism will rely."'

Liebermann had handed the photograph album back to Lance, who looked once again at the picture of the Schneiders posing with their son. Mummy and Daddy looked like nice, ordinary people, and their son looked like a nice ordinary boy. What a world that had been . . .

'What happened to the Schneiders?'

'Rudolf was killed in action on the Eastern Front near the end of the war. Helga committed suicide while in prison in Leipzig. Somebody on the outside smuggled in a capsule of potassium cyanide. It was thought that she had personally murdered a Jewish shopkeeper during Kristallnacht.'

'And the boy?'

'The boy's in that file, too. Franz Schneider volunteered to join the SS in 1942 when he was eighteen and became a guard at the Stutthof concentration camp. For one so young, he was renowned for his brutality. He regarded all the prisoners as sub-human and treated them accordingly. Towards the end of the war, he disappeared from Stutthof, and it was rumoured, but never proved, that he had murdered one of his superior officers and an SS-Unterscharfuhrer.'

Liebermann dragged another faded sheet of paper from the file.

'Here it is. SS-Sturmbannfuhrer Egon Scharnhorst and SS-Unterscharfuhrer Alois Schmidt. The camp was understaffed, and the German civilian police were asked to investigate. Witnesses told how Franz Schneider had been in the same isolated part of the camp as the two victims at the time when it was presumed they had been killed, but by this time Schneider himself had gone missing. Both men had been stabbed in the heart, most likely by a ceremonial SS dagger.'

Lance shivered. 'The same fate suffered a lifetime later by Sir Frank Taylor. Frank Taylor, Franz Schneider . . .'

'Frank and Franz are the same name. And "Schneider" is German for "tailor". But I think I have something here that could well lay those disturbing thoughts to rest.'

He took another sheet from the folder.

'This is a police report dated 16 April 1945, made by a detective officer of the Orpo, the civilian police force, working out of their headquarters in Danzig. It tells us that the body of a young man in SS uniform was found stabbed to death in the snow on a road leading into Danzig. It was a few days after a death march from Stutthof concentration camp comprising five hundred prisoners and a posse of SS guards. A search of the young man's body found his party card and identity documents in his pocket. They both stated that he was Franz Schneider.'

'What happened to the five hundred prisoners?'

'When they reached Danzig Harbour, they were driven into the water and machine gunned.'

The two men were silent for a moment. Neither had been born when the Third Reich fell, but in some obscure way they both felt that they, too, were its victims. Their lives were permanently sullied by knowledge of the outrages that had been committed in the not-too-distant past.

'So, it's a dead end,' said Lance, at length. 'Franz Schneider was not our Sir Frank Taylor.'

'Well, maybe so, but it leaves an intriguing question unanswered. Why was that photograph album kept all those years by Sir Frank Taylor? If he wasn't once Franz Schneider, surely it had no sentimental value? I'm not sure there's much more I can do to help with this, but if you like, I'll have the documents I've shown you photocopied, and released from embargo?'

Liebermann once again examined the passport through his hand lens.

'There's a scar under his chin, perhaps the result of a childhood injury. Did Sir Frank Taylor have a similar scar?'

'No, though the doctor who conducted the autopsy said that it could have faded completely over the course of his long lifetime.'

'Hm . . . Another dead end, then.' He glanced back at the documents Lance had brought him. 'Or maybe not? These documents show that Sir Frank Taylor once made quite a substantial donation to the Danzig Old Comrades' Association. The association was a front organization for spiriting wanted Nazis out of Germany and into Latin America. It still exists and is patronized by old men crying into their beer and longing for the old days. The BKA still keep a wary eye on them.' He reached for a piece of paper and pen.

'I'm going to put you in touch with a man called Dr Aaron Koestler, who works at the Leo Baeck Institute, here in Berlin. The institute specializes in research into the history of German Jewry from the age of the Enlightenment to the outbreak of the Second World War. Dr Koestler has made it his purpose in life to enquire into the fates of long-forgotten Jews whose lives were either disrupted or ended by the Holocaust. Can you stay another day in Berlin? Because this man will almost certainly be able to resurrect the early history of Chaim Jakob Shapiro.'

* * *

Lance found Dr Aaron Koestler in a three-storey modern building behind the Jewish Museum in Linden Strasse, part of the Leo Baeck Institute. He was a small, bald man, wearing a light fawn suit over a white shirt and a polka-dotted bow tie. He peered at his visitor through thick-lensed glasses.

'Herr Liebermann rang me last night to say that you would come this morning,' he said. 'You have a passport that he said would interest me.' He spoke quietly, in what Lance recognized as a southern German accent. His manner was that of a grave academic. 'May I see the passport?'

Koestler motioned to Lance to draw up a chair beside him at his desk. His fingers flitted rapidly over the keyboard of his computer, and when he was presented with a text box, he typed in the name Chaim Jakob Shapiro, and pressed 'enter'. The screen replied with a message: *10 matches found.* Koestler clicked his tongue in annoyance.

'We know from a collection of letters we found,' said Lance, 'that he lived at one time in Mannheim, in Baden-Wurttemberg.' Once more the busy fingers flew over the keys.

'Ah! Here's our man!' Koestler cried. 'Our researchers recovered him more than ten years ago. Let me bring up his dossier . . .' A few moments later what was evidently a scanned copy of an original paper document appeared on the screen.

'Shapiro family of Mannheim. Alphonse Moses Shapiro, timber exporter. His wife, Anna Shapiro, *née* Goldberg. Son, Chaim Jakob Shapiro . . . All the dates and ages are given here. Chaim was born in 1924, so he'd have been fourteen when his passport photograph was taken. Family arrested by Gestapo 11 May 1942. All three sent to Stutthof Concentration Camp, 16 May. Ascertained from other sources that all three were sent to the gas chamber only days after their admission to the camp. I can find out more?'

'I want to hear as much as I can,' said Lance. 'A picture is beginning to emerge in my mind — a picture I don't much like.'

Dr Koestler moved to another console and summoned up further information on the fate of the Shapiro family.

'Here we are,' he said. 'This is a photo-scan of the camp doctor's report on a whole batch of "items" received at the camp in May 1942. They called Jews "items" you know. "Two hundred items received today." That kind of thing. We were not regarded as human beings.' A spasm of anger crossed the academic's face, but it was gone in a moment. 'The doctor examined these three particular items, listed here as "Jew Israel Alphonse Moses Shapiro, Jewess Sara Anna Shapiro, and Jew Israel Chaim Jakob Shapiro." All male Jews had to take the name Israel, and all Jewesses the name Sara. It was all part of the nightmare.' He scrolled down the page. '"All three Shapiros are suffering from different stages of tuberculosis. Chaim Jakob Shapiro, born 1924, has evidently had a small tubercular tumour removed from his neck. All three are unfit for the work programme followed here and should be disposed of as soon as it is convenient.

Tubercular prisoners pose a grave danger to other prisoners, as tuberculosis is a contagious disease."

'So there it is, Mr Middleton. The unspeakable fate of the Shapiro family of Mannheim. Blotted out. They have no graves, no known resting place. But their memory lives on in databases like these, and in the memorials at Yad Vashem. I have brought back literally thousands of people like the Shapiros to the memory of all those living now. That little family is no longer entirely forgotten.'

Koestler threw off his retrospective manner and returned to matters of the moment.

'The question remains: how did the young man's passport survive, and who was it who made use of it after the war?'

'Our knowledge is partial, at best. The passport was used by a man who later changed his name to Frank Taylor — he left Germany and became a naturalized British citizen. He has recently passed away, and I've been tasked with finding out more about this document.'

'Well, it's now evident that this Frank Taylor and Chaim Jakob Shapiro could not have been the same person. It could be that Frank Taylor was himself a Jewish refugee, but one who made his escape from Germany using the discarded passport of Chaim Jakob Shapiro. He may have had no identity documents of his own, and acquired Chaim's passport from someone at Stutthof. Things like that did happen. But it's still a mystery.'

13. BROTHER ANSELM'S CONFESSION

The serene beauty of the countryside in that part of the Rhineland-Palatinate where the Priory of Kloster Eisenbach was situated enraptured Lance Middleton. It was a land of fertile vineyards and gently flowing streams, high wooded slopes and rocky eminences. The chauffeured Mercedes-Benz made its way through picturesque villages, past fairy-tale castles perched high above rivers, and so into the remote valley where the Benedictine Priory of Kloster Eisenbach clung to its wooded inland cliff.

Lance had hired the car and driver in Mainz, and had been able to sit back and think of the mission that he had accepted. He came armed with little more than an old passport and a briefcase full of photocopies of documents relevant to the life of a man called Chaim Jakob Shapiro, and to the life of another man, known in England for a lifetime as Sir Frank Taylor. He came armed, too, with fluent German, which went beyond text-book knowledge: he could understand most of the dialects spoken in Germany, and was thus confident when speaking to people who might have been ill at ease attempting conversations in faltering English.

The driver stopped at an ornate baroque gate, and pointed up to the priory, where onion domes and slender spires seemed to touch the clouds.

'There's no road for cars beyond this point, *mein Herr*,' he said with a half-smile, noting his portly customer's dismay. 'But there is a phone here, in the wall, and if you state your business, they'll send someone down with the donkey-cart to take you up to the priory.'

After a lapse of twenty minutes or so, a cart pulled by a diminutive donkey, appeared on the other side of the gate. It was driven by a spare, sun-bronzed man in the black habit of a Benedictine monk, who helped Lance to fit himself into the little vehicle. His driver turned the Mercedes-Benz in the road and drove off to the village below.

The little donkey toiled upward through groves of trees, where Lance could see rows of well-tended beehives.

Eventually, they passed through a gap in the trees, and there before him Lance saw the front aspect of the fanciful building that had been engraved on the priory's letterhead. Hopefully, someone inside this mysterious building would be able to tell him the truth about Chaim Jakob Shapiro and the late world-renowned actor, Sir Frank Taylor.

On the stroke of twelve, as the Angelus rang out from one of the bell towers, a great nail-studded door seemed to open as if by magic, and the monk turned the little donkey-cart round and moved away out of sight. Despite his best efforts, Lance could not rid himself of the feeling that he was Jonathan Harker, arriving at Castle Dracula to meet the Undead.

Another monk stepped out to greet him, an alert man in his fifties, wearing rimless glasses, which reminded Lance of Detective Inspector French.

'Welcome to Kloster Eisenbach, Herr Middleton,' said the monk, smiling and shaking hands. 'I am Prior Kraus. Let's go to my office. We can talk in privacy there.'

They walked along quiet, cool passages and up time-worn flights of steps until they came to the prior's office on the second floor, where a great ebony crucifix adorned one of the stone walls.

The prior motioned to Lance to sit in one of two chairs on either side of a massive stone fireplace containing an arrangement of spring flowers and leaves.

'It's a warm day, Herr Middleton,' said the prior. 'Let me pour you a glass of one of our celebrated vintages.'

It was indeed a superb Rhenish wine, cool and rich. Lance relaxed in his chair.

'Where are all your brethren, Father Prior?' he asked. 'I've only seen one, besides yourself, and he didn't have much to say for himself.'

'That was Brother Wilhelm,' said the prior, smiling. 'He's not very fond of words. As for the others, they're all out at work in the vineyards and the brewery. They'll all be back here mid-afternoon for the Divine Office.'

The prior shifted in his chair, and it was as if, by doing so, he had left the world of polite conversation for more serious, and possibly more sinister, things.

'You have come here to uncover secrets,' he said, 'secrets that would be better left buried. If I can assure you that some truths are best left untold, will you return to England? No, your expression tells me that you would do no such thing.'

'Truth, Father Prior,' said Lance, 'has always struggled to break through the seductive power of darkness and lies. You know that better than I do. Back in England I left a man of ninety-four murdered — stabbed — by someone with strong links to Germany's past. I think the clue to his murderer lies here, in Eisenbach. Does not his murder demand justice?'

Prior Kraus sighed, resigned.

'You are right,' he said, 'of course you are right. I will take you now to Brother Anselm, and leave you with him. He, too, is ninety-four, and very frail, but he is ready to tell his frightful story before he dies. Indeed, I think he's been keeping himself alive in order to do so. He has told it all to me in confession, where, of course, it remains a secret between the two of us, but I have withheld absolution until he has assured me, this very day, that he had told you that story, too. He's in the infirmary.'

Brother Anselm lay in an iron cot in one of a number of single rooms in the modern infirmary building of Kloster Eisenbach. There were no monks around, only a white-coated doctor, his stethoscope draped around his neck.

Lance Middleton could see at a glance that the old man was perilously close to death. He lay quite still, his gnarled hands lying motionless on the coverlet. The skin of his face was parchment thin, giving the illusion that his cheekbones would very soon burst through his flesh.

'Anselm,' said the prior, 'this is Herr Middleton. He has my authority to hear your story. When you have finished telling him all that you told me under the seal of confession, I will come and give you absolution.' He motioned to the doctor, and both men left the room, closing the door behind them. The dying monk looked searchingly at Lance through faded grey eyes, and then began to speak in a low but clear voice.

'They were terrible days, days of endless suffering without any hope of release. It was as though we had all been con-demned to live in hell on earth, prisoners and guards alike. My name in those days was Klaus Heinemann, and my great friend was Franz Schneider. We had been at school together and continued to look out for each other even in the Stutthof concentration camp.'

Brother Anselm stopped speaking for a moment, as though the effort to tell his story was proving too much.

'It was in early 1945,' Anselm continued, 'that Franz and I began to plan our escape. Franz was the leader always — he'd been so at school and had planned to become a teacher before the war changed the course of both of our lives for ever. There was a forced march planned for 13 February, a march of twenty miles from Stutthof to Danzig. My plan was to slip away from the march as we entered Danzig, and to stow away on a merchant ship leaving for one of the Nordic countries.

'Franz had other ideas. Everybody in that camp was desperate and dangerous, and in order to carry out his plan, which was to escape to the West behind British or American lines, he would have to kill his way out.'

The old man uttered an involuntary sob, and tears rolled down his cheeks.

'That is what happens to you in a place like Stutthof,' he continued. 'Living with death and the threat of death every day, you lose all sense of normal morality.

'Franz Schneider had two dangerous enemies in that camp. One was SS-Sturmbannfuhrer Egon Scharnhorst, a brute of a man who had been a butcher in civilian life, and his toady, Unterscharfuhrer Alois Schmidt. They knew all about Franz's perfect English, and resented his being educationally superior to them, so whenever there was any particularly unpleasant task to be performed, they made sure that Franz was involved in it. He would be made to stand in the freezing cold while those two chatted about trivia. They were both hateful men.

'On the night before the forced march, Franz told me that he intended to "neutralize" his two enemies, in case they tried to interfere with his plan by suddenly taking him off the march at the last moment, and making him do something else. They had both done things like that to him before.

'So that is what he did. He pretended to ingratiate himself with both of them, saying that he could get them a couple of bottles of vodka if they'd come to the electric fence behind the crematorium at one o'clock that night. They took the bait, and when they arrived at the rendezvous, he and another man — I never found out who it was — stabbed them both to the heart.'

'And this man — Franz Schneider — became Sir Frank Taylor? He killed . . .' Lance's voice faltered.

'You can have no idea what it was like, living in those times,' said Brother Anselm. 'It was a different world. Different principles applied.'

'Yes,' Lance conceded, 'I can well believe it. I don't condone murder of any kind, but Frank — Franz — had seen so many of his own Jewish people butchered.'

The old man gave a dreadful cry, and reared up on the bed.

'Oh, my God! You have misunderstood, all this time. I thought you knew. Franz Schneider and I were not prisoners. *We were SS guards!*

SS guards. The words echoed dimly in Lance's head. And with a sickening lurch of his stomach, he knew it to be true. *How had he not seen it until now?* Sir Frank was no hapless victim — a nameless refugee in search of a fresh start — he was a monster hiding in plain sight.

'There was a room at Stutthof,' Brother Anselm continued, 'a vile corridor of a place, where the doors at either end were always blowing open, letting in the snow and rain. It was here that the prisoners' suitcases and other belongings were plundered for money and jewellery. Special groups of prisoners, many of them jewellers in their vanished lives, sat on the wet floor, searching the linings of cases, ripping open coats, prising the heels off shoes . . . Everything else was thrown away, to be trodden underfoot as fresh batches of loot were brought in to be processed.

'Franz was utterly ruthless. He treated all prisoners as sub-humans, lashing out and beating anyone who caused him the slightest annoyance. I wasn't like that. I had too much imagination not to be upset by what I saw, though I never let anyone see that.'

'Are you excusing yourself?' asked Lance Middleton. 'You tell me that you were an SS guard, too. You were as bad as Franz Schneider.'

'No, I was not! I did my duty, and that was all, but Franz was cruel and vindictive. And in any case, I paid dearly for my role as an SS guard, as I will tell you, if you care to listen.

'And so one afternoon Franz and I came to the chilly wet corridor where the prisoners' effects were plundered and profaned. The concrete floor was swimming with water, and floating in it were the discarded remnants of obliterated lives, family photographs, marriage certificates, intimate letters, photographs of men in smart suits and women in pretty

140

dresses, men in uniform, with the Iron Cross pinned to their chest, and children, children . . . All rendered anonymous, deprived of names and given tattooed numbers, all of them reduced to handfuls of ashes.'

Lance Middleton said nothing. He had been staring in fascination at the old man's wizened right arm, where a tattooed number was still clearly discernible. What could that mean? Brother Anselm followed his eyes, and knew what he had seen.

'I kept that number as part of my atonement,' he said. 'That is my SS membership number — many of us had it tattooed on our arms, because the party and the SS were to last for ever. Franz had his number also tattooed on his arm, but as soon as he could after his escape, he had it burned off with acid. He was more fanatical about changing his identity than I was — he told me, years later, in one of his letters to me, that he had paid one of the few rabbis who had survived the Holocaust to arrange for him to receive a Jewish ritual circumcision. Franz Schneider was to disappear completely from history, and Chaim Jakob Shapiro was to take his place. But when he looked around for an English name, his vanity made him anglicize his real German name to Frank Taylor.'

Lance Middleton was generally an amiable man, but on this occasion his indignation made him speak brutally.

'You say he was able to pay a rabbi. Did Franz also steal money and jewels from the dead?'

'He took some money, yes, and some items of jewellery that he removed from the dead body of Major Scharnhorst, who was a thief on a grand scale. All money and jewels were to be sent back to Berlin, but a lot of it found its way into Major Scharnhorst's ample pockets.'

Another sob convulsed the old man's frame, but he seemed to be driven by some inner compulsion to continue his story.

'I told you how we went to the waterlogged corridor, and what we saw there. Franz picked up two passports, both half soaked, and one stained with blood.'

Lance produced Chaim's passport from an inside pocket, and held it in front of the dying man's eyes.

'That's it. That is the passport that Franz decided to keep. How did you find it? He said it would be his passport to freedom. We both knew the Third Reich was doomed, and we were only in our early twenties. Franz offered me the other passport that he'd picked up, but I couldn't take it. What name is written on it? Chaim Jakob Shapiro. Poor boy! He looks quite like the young Franz in that photograph, which is, I suppose, why he chose it. And so it became his passport to freedom, and to a new life as Sir Frank Taylor. I saw him in *Charlemagne*. I couldn't believe that it was Franz.'

'Tell me about the escape.'

'We set off at first light on 13 April. It was a Friday. There were five hundred prisoners, and either six or eight of us guards, I can't remember the exact number. But we were all armed to the teeth and stronger by far. It was bitterly cold, and although it was April, deep snow covered the ground. The forced march was one of twenty miles. The bodies of those two men were not discovered until long after we had left the camp, I found out later.'

'There's something about those days that I can tell you,' said Lance Middleton, 'though perhaps I'm telling you something that you already know. I have seen a report made by the Orpo, the civilian German police, and dated 16 April 1945, which says that the body of a young man in SS uniform was found stabbed to death in the snow on a road leading into Danzig. A search of the young man's body found his party card and identity documents in his pocket. They both stated that he was Franz Schneider.'

The old man's voice was growing fainter, but Lance could hear quite clearly what he said.

'Yes. Somewhere along the way, he murdered one of the other guards and planted his own identity papers on him. The guard's own papers he destroyed. Franz didn't want to be identified as German, you see. He was my friend, and remained a friend for life, but he was a ruthless man, and a devoted Nazi.

'And so, some miles before we were supposed to arrive at Danzig, Franz slipped away from the detail and made his way to the West. He told me in a letter that he had broken into a deserted house and changed his uniform for civilian clothing. And so he escaped to the West as Chaim Jakob Shapiro, and became a great British actor. He tried to forget his early life, and told me once that he had become an entirely different person. But of course he hadn't, and when the time was ripe they came after him.'

'They? Who were these people?'

'They are an underground, nameless organization doling out retribution to people whom they branded as traitors to the Fatherland. Franz Schneider — Frank Taylor — was such a one. I heard from a man who used to visit me here from time to time that one of their number had been a "sleeper" in England for a number of years, waiting for the time to avenge the murders of Major Scharnhorst and Unterscharfuhrer Schmidt. I contrived to warn Franz, but it seems that I was too late.'

'Who was this assassin? What is his name?'

'I don't know. Nobody will know. But there you have the whole terrible story of my friend Franz Schneider.'

The old man fell quiet, and he closed his eyes. For one tense moment Lance thought that he had died. But there was something that the dying man had wanted to tell him, and it was his duty to hear him out. He gently touched Brother Anselm's hand, and his eyes opened.

'What happened to you?' asked Lance. 'How did you come to be here?'

'I followed my original plan, which was to stow away on one of the Baltic ships at Danzig. I had thrown away my own identity papers, and would claim to be a displaced person. Europe was in turmoil, and it was possible to succeed in passing yourself off as an innocent victim of the Nazis. I planned to steal some civilian clothing as soon as an opportunity offered. O Lord, forgive us! Our movement was born in lies, and perished in lies . . .

'My story is soon told. The Russians were everywhere, and I was soon seized as an enemy soldier, and sent to a holding camp in what had been Brandenburg. I was eventually hauled up before a military court, where a few scarecrow remnants of those liberated from Stutthof gave evidence against me. I was sentenced to eight years in the gulag. I returned to Germany in 1953, a physical and mental wreck.'

'How did you become a monk?'

'When I returned to Leipzig, everything was still in ruins. Of my family there was no trace: I never found out what happened to them. I was reduced to beggary until I was rescued by a Catholic charitable order, the Brothers of the Divine Compassion. It was they who restored me to physical and mental health, and rekindled the Catholicism that had lain latent from my childhood. I entered the order, and took final vows in 1964.

'Franz and I kept up a fairly regular correspondence — we had become virtually two different people from the young men who had served in the SS. When I turned ninety, I began to suffer from various lingering ailments, and I was sent here to this Benedictine house to see out my days. Soon, Father Prior will give me absolution. What I ask you now, Herr Middleton, is this: do *you* forgive me?'

Lance Middleton was silent for a while, sensing Anselm's longing. This dying man had been a child at the start of the war, brought up to believe in an unspeakable ideology. But it took a particularly terrible psychology, he reminded himself, to actually volunteer for the SS, to separate families, to murder little babies and elderly men much like the one before him, simply for existing. Yet that was what the SS guards in concentration camps had done, without exception. And, in telling his story, Anselm had made every effort to excuse his actions, to play them down. He hadn't really accepted his own guilt. What could Lance say in response?

'It isn't my place to forgive you, Brother Anselm,' he said. 'You must ask that of the relatives of the men, women and children you murdered in the camps. And there are those in England who will bring the killer of Sir Frank Taylor to justice. Taylor may have been a killer himself, many times over, but in my country, Brother Anselm, we don't condone murder.'

He briefly squeezed the old man's hand before leaving him, as the prior, with a purple stole around his neck, came in to give the former SS guard absolution.

Lance had just reached the entrance of the priory when a bell began to toll, signalling that Brother Anselm had died.

14. A DEATH IN DOVER STREET FLATS

'Terry Lucas was a fool,' said DI French. 'It's clear from our interrogations that he thought he had the potential to be a criminal mastermind, when in fact he was little more than a go-between for greater and more depraved minds than his own. We still haven't found Sagawa — I wouldn't be surprised if he's fled the country.'

Glyn laughed.

The two detectives were in DI French's office. The eighteenth of May was proving to be very warm, and the windows were open. They could both hear the fractious beeping of horns in the town hall car park.

'When are we going to move against Balonek, sir?'

'As soon as we find out whether or not his grandfather was really in the Free Polish Forces. If he wasn't, then presumably Teddy Balonek isn't all he appears to be. But we mustn't make a premature move, Glyn. After all, we still don't know why he wanted to harm old Sir Frank Taylor. Let's leave him in happy ignorance of our suspicions for the moment.'

DI French sat back in his chair and looked at his sergeant with a kind of curious speculation.

'Glyn,' said DI French, 'something has happened to you since you took those two days' leave. You seem to have perked up, if that's the right expression. You're more the man I first spotted when you were still in uniform. What have you been up to?'

'Sir, I found out that Sandra — my wife — has been suffering from mental health problems for over two years. She's seeing a doctor and I've a renewed commitment to her, and that includes doing my part, instead of drowning in self-pity. I'm redecorating, and making the house fit for Sandra when she returns from her mother's. I'm eating properly, too.'

'That's marvellous news, Glyn. I knew something was up, but didn't know it was as serious as that. Does her mother know?'

'Oh, yes. Her mother's a good sort, you know. So it's almost as though Sandra and I are starting all over again. And this time, everything's going to work out for the very best. We might even—'

There was a knock on French's door, and a uniformed constable came into the office.

'Sir,' he said, 'there's been a suspected suicide in Dover Street, in one of those riverside flats by the canal. An elderly man. Dr Dunwoody wants you to go there now. He thinks it might be something to do with Sir Frank Taylor's murder.'

Dover Street lay in a part of the town that was allegedly 'waiting for development'. Two blocks of pre-war flats stood in an overgrown communal garden on the right bank of the disused, and now stagnant, canal. French had seen the proposed plans for the area, architects' drawings of people sitting out on terraces, sipping cocktails, with elegant modern apartments rising behind them. The county council occasionally mentioned the 'Canal-side Project', but everybody knew that nothing would ever come of it.

Police cars stood outside the left-hand block of flats, their lights still flashing. A uniformed sergeant took French and Edwards into the building. The lift was out of order, and they began the climb up to the fifth floor. Residents could be seen flitting away on the landings as they walked up.

'It's a sad business, sir,' said the sergeant, a young man who had begun to experiment with a beard. 'A neighbour found him about an hour ago, when she called on him with some shopping. He looks about eighty, a little bald man, lying dead in his bed.'

'And have you ascertained the man's name?' DI French preferred his professional corpses to be referred to as 'the decedent'.

'Yes, sir. He was a Mr Josef Schmidt. The neighbour said he's lived here for over twenty years.'

They could smell the scent of bitter almonds as soon as they entered the bedroom of the cramped, sparsely furnished flat. Both men knew what that meant. Ray Dunwoody was sitting on a chair bedside the bed.

'I've composed his limbs,' he began without preamble, 'but when I found him it was obvious to me that he'd suffered convulsions following the ingestion of cyanide. You can still detect the typical smell of bitter almonds. He committed suicide.'

DI French had taken in the dead man's flat at a glance. It had been the home of a man of limited means, but not someone without a sufficient income. There was a living room, kitchen, bedroom and bathroom, all quite neat and clean.

'Why did you bring us here, Ray? Suicide is sad, but it's not a crime.'

'Mr Schmidt had not swallowed a cyanide capsule or drunk the poison in one of its liquid forms. He had bitten down upon a false tooth which contained the poison. Here it is. I removed it from his mouth. From the condition of the inner lining, which is made of gold, I should say that the implant had been in his gum for many years.'

DI French looked at the false tooth as it lay in the palm of his hand.

'This is the kind of thing that spies used to have during the war,' he said.

'It is,' said Dunwoody. 'When I was studying forensics, I attended a course on these devices, given by the Army

Intelligence Corps at Maresfield. That's why I can tell you that this was the type of implant used by the Abwehr, the Nazis' secret intelligence service. I think we have just found the man who murdered Sir Frank Taylor.'

DI French was non-committal. It was very tempting to leap to that kind of conclusion, but he would want more positive evidence than that. Successful assassins didn't usually commit suicide. As if in answer to his doubts, Glyn, who had been searching the living room, put a sheet of paper into his hand.

'He left a confession of sorts,' he said. 'It was just lying on the windowsill.'

After a lifetime's patient waiting, I failed in my mission. Someone else got there before me and sent Franz Schneider on his way to hell. Someone else avenged the murders of Egon Scharnhorst and Alois Schmidt, my grandfather. — Josef Schmidt.

'Old sins cast long shadows,' said DI French. 'This man was harbouring thoughts of revenge for a lifetime, and had been fitted with a cyanide capsule in case his mission failed — and he had been here, living quietly in Oldminster — for years, and we never knew. Glyn, make a thorough search of these premises, but I don't think you'll find anything much of interest. Mr Schmidt evidently kept things close to his chest.'

'Yes, sir,' said DS Edwards, 'it's a dead end, if you'll pardon the expression. And we still have no idea who murdered Sir Frank Taylor — or why.'

* * *

The next morning, DI French received a fax from the cultural attaché at the Polish Embassy.

Dear Inspector French, I can confirm that a Mateusz Balonek served as a detective inspector in the Polish Criminal Police until 1945, and was retained as a police officer in the post-war years, including the early years of the Communist regime. His son, Jan, and the son's wife, Wanda, emigrated to England, living initially in London. They had one child, Tadeusz, born in England. Always known as Teddy, he trained as a chef. He speaks Polish and German, as well as English, which he regards as his native language. His parents are both dead, and he is unmarried. I hope these facts will be of use to you.

A pattern was beginning to emerge. For some obscure reason, buried in the past, some amorphous group or groups wanted revenge on Sir Frank Taylor. One group had been represented by the old man found dead in Dover Street flats. He had a German name and was bent on avenging the deaths of a Major Scharnhorst, and also of his own grandfather, someone called Alois Schmidt. It was probably time to enlist the help of the Foreign Office, but if they made moves in that direction, then Scotland Yard would insist on being involved.

Old Mr Schmidt had considered himself as a failure, and had committed suicide when someone else beat him to it. Why had he waited so long? He may have been an ineffective ditherer, putting off his mission as day succeeded day, and year followed year. He'd come across people like that. Prevaricators.

But it looked as though there were other people after Frank Taylor's blood, as someone — someone still unknown — had murdered him. The killer had to have been on the premises on the night that Sir Frank was murdered. Setting aside the ludicrous idea that Nurse Trickett had done the deed, Teddy Balonek was the only other resident staff member living in the main house, and Teddy Balonek had a family timeline reaching back to the collaborationist Polish Criminal Police. It was time to move against Teddy, before he smelled a rat and made himself scarce.

* * *

As Glyn emerged from Boot's in Oldminster high street, he bumped into Mervyn Sanders, the reputable antiques dealer.

'Why, Detective Sergeant Edwards!' Mervyn said, extending a hand. 'How nice to see you. Have you made any further progress? About the murder of Sir Frank Taylor, I mean.'

The two men fell in step, as they were both going in the direction of the town hall.

'We're pursuing various lines of enquiry, Mr Sanders,' said Glyn.

The antiques dealer laughed.

'You have to say that, don't you? It's like when some murderer is caught in the act, and it says in the paper, "A man will appear in court today." A man! It's all such solemn nonsense. About that dagger, Sergeant. Are you sure it's not for sale? I'll raise my offer to £500.'

'That's very generous of you, Mr Sanders, but I'm afraid it's not ours to sell. In any case, it's Exhibit A, ready to be produced in court when we eventually catch Sir Frank's killer.'

Mervyn stopped as they reached the town hall and put a hand on Glyn's arm. Glyn looked at him in alarm: he had suddenly gone pale, and his hand was trembling.

'As regards Sir Frank's killer,' Mervyn said, 'my theory is that it must have been an inside job. Either one of the residents did it, or one of the live-in staff. What about that Pole? Balonek? *He* lives in—'

'Are you offering me incriminating information about Mr Balonek?'

'Well, no, but he does live in, doesn't he? I'd look into his antecedents, if I were you.' And without another word, he turned and hurried off.

* * *

Charles Forshaw sat in the common room at the Irving Home for Retired Actors, finishing the *Daily Telegraph* cryptic crossword. It was a quiet time in the afternoon, when most of the residents were taking a nap. Tony Hayling was out in the grounds, determined to take his daily walk. Tony had once confided to him that he dreaded the thought of ending up in a wheelchair and took what exercise he could.

Poor old Frank, he'd left them all a thousand pounds each. He'd use his gift to have a new monument made for Coretta's grave in Kensal Green Cemetery, a marble angel, arms outstretched to heaven, the features modelled on Coretta's face as she had been in her prime. He went to Kensal Green four times a year with offerings of her favourite flowers, and he would tell her all the latest theatrical news. But her headstone was leaning, and some of the letters had fallen off. The great Coretta Grierson deserved something better than that.

Charles put down the paper and glanced around the room. His eyes rested on what had been Frank's chair, though he always remarked testily that 'we don't have our own special chairs'.

Frank . . . His instinct told him he was murdered by someone who was actually in the house that night. But who? He cast his mind back to the evening of Frank's death, what they had all done, and what they had talked about. And then suddenly, with a gut-wrenching shock, he knew.

He walked out into the deserted entrance hall. Trudy Vosper wasn't there, so he was able to rummage through the papers on the reception desk without fear of interruption. Yes, there it was, as clear as daylight. That alone, produced as evidence in court, would seal the killer's fate.

What should he do? The obvious thing would be to tell Detective Inspector French. But he had always been a fair-minded man. Should he not at least give the suspect the chance of telling his side of the story? He permitted himself a wry amused smile. Tony Hayling had very effectively made himself a celebrity by his lurid memoirs, currently appearing in a national newspaper. Why shouldn't *he* have his moment of glory? Sometime next week, he'd surprise them all by revealing how old Frank had been murdered, and who it was that had murdered him.

* * *

That evening, Glyn called in to the Grapes for a pint of lager. The pub seemed to hold a renewed interest for him. He admired the pictures on the walls, which he'd never really noticed before, and enjoyed the sparkling welcome of the many polished glasses hanging above the bar. He realized that this pub was no longer a refuge from his sorrows, but a nice place to visit.

He looked around the bar, and spotted Marie. She was in animated conversation with a very good-looking man who was cradling a pint while he listened to her talk. She had ordered her usual port and lemon, or maybe her friend had bought it for her.

He suddenly felt a chill in his stomach. If he had not found out about Sandra when he did, he could very easily have tried it on with Marie. He would always like her, but she no longer posed a temptation to him. She looked up, caught his eye, and waved cheerfully at him. Glyn heard her companion whisper, 'Who's he?' and after she'd replied to him he, too, turned and gave him a cheery wave. Glyn finished his pint and stood up. Time to go home.

* * *

Bosszuallo had always known the voices in his head were not *normal*. But he'd assumed they came from some dark corner of his own psyche. Now he wasn't so sure. Was it his own voice? Or that of a *demon*? Whispering things to him, urging him to fulfil his destiny as Bosszuallo, the Avenger. He'd tried to resist, but was always vanquished. He had once taken advice from someone he trusted and had gone secretly to consult a psychiatrist in Chichester. It had been a frightening experience. The psychiatrist had warned him that heeding the voices in his head could lead to him committing acts that he would later regret — he called such incidents 'psychotic episodes'. Could he be cured? Yes, said the psychiatrist, but it would take some time, with the necessity of regular counselling. Drugs? Some forms of medication were certainly possible, but they would be a last resort.

While the man was speaking, a voice in his head told him quite clearly: 'This man is your enemy. Can't you see that in his eyes? He is one of Franz Schneider's friends.'

He had mumbled some excuse, and had taken his leave, the psychiatrist begging him to reconsider. But the voice had told him: 'He wants your money, but more than that, he wants your soul.'

Bosszuallo sat at his computer in the upstairs room, and made contact with Msciciel, pleading for help. Msciciel told him that although his mission had been successfully accomplished, there was always more work for him to do, if he wished to accept it. There were still many unavenged, and if he remained true to his vocation, and heeded what the voices told him, he could banish his doubts and fears through further direct action. Meanwhile, watch and wait. There were enemies everywhere, waiting to pounce.

15. TEDDY BALONEK'S STATEMENT

When Lance Middleton arrived at Oldminster train station, he found Noel waiting for him in his Ford Mondeo. As usual, Lance fussed and fretted about his journey back to England by British Airways — he could have caught a later Lufthansa flight, with all its well-known comforts, but felt that he needed to get back to England as soon as possible.

He continued his chatter as he squeezed his ample bulk into the car, this time complaining about the traffic in London, while Noel loaded his luggage into the boot. There was a locked black leather briefcase, and what Lance Middleton liked to call his 'overnight valise'; evidently he was expecting Noel to put him up for the night, which of course he would do.

Noel Greenspan and Chloe McArthur lived in flats on opposite sides of Wellington Square, a rather battered Regency gem in the area east of Cathedral Green. There was a railed garden in the centre of the square, and at one time the residents had had their own keys to open the gates. However, since all the properties in Wellington Square had long ago been converted to flats and offices, the garden was more or less public property.

The chatter ceased as Noel brought the car to a halt on Chloe's side of the square. Lance had become uncharacteristically quiet, and when he greeted Chloe with his familiar perfunctory kiss, he failed to add the barrage of compliments that usually accompanied it. Although very tempting savoury smells came from the gas-fired Aga, the gourmet seemed not to notice. He sat down at the kitchen table and unlocked the black briefcase.

'Chloe and Noel,' he said, 'I have been entirely successful in establishing the true identity of Chaim Jakob Shapiro and Sir Frank Taylor. Shapiro was a young man who perished with his parents at the Stutthof concentration camp, near Dresden. Frank Taylor, *alias* Franz Schneider, was an SS camp guard.'

While Noel and Chloe sat in appalled silence, Lance Middleton gave then a full account of his visit to Berlin, and his subsequent journey to the remote priory of Kloster Eisenbach.

'We were seeing everything from the wrong angle,' said Lance. 'Frank Taylor was not a victim — he was one of the oppressors. Like his parents, he was a fanatical Nazi, cruel and inhuman in his treatment of the inmates of that camp, and when he saw that his side was going to lose the war, he murdered his way to freedom. He buried his old life as deeply as he could, but there were others harbouring an equally deep desire for vengeance. It was one of their agents who murdered him at the Irving Home for Retired Actors.'

Looking disturbed at the awful news, Chloe McArthur rose from the table and busied herself at the Aga, spooning coffee into the stovetop percolator.

'I promised Charles Forshaw that I'd keep him posted about this,' said Noel.

'Do so by all means,' said Lance, 'but not before I've placed all my findings before Detective Inspector French and Sergeant Edwards. I've already texted French to make an appointment to see them first thing tomorrow morning.' Chloe placed the coffee and biscuits on the table. 'Oh, thank you, Chloe, that's very welcome. I apologize for not being my usual scintillating self today. What I learned in Germany shocked me.'

'What did you make of this old monk, this Brother Anselm?'

'On the surface, he appeared repentant, true enough, but he seemed to me more fixated on his own suffering than that of the people he'd put to harm. He'd spent years in the gulag, followed by a lifetime as a monk. I could afford the luxury of feeling rather sorry for him. That's the danger of meeting monsters in the flesh. And he filled in the gaps about the celebrated late actor Sir Frank Taylor: a ruthless killer, who murdered his way to fame and fortune.'

'Still, he was murdered himself,' said Noel Greenspan, 'and his murderer hasn't yet been brought to justice. His killers waited a lifetime, but vengeance runs deep.'

'That Nazi dagger, the dagger that was used to kill him,' said Lance, 'was Frank's own, a fond souvenir of his days as an executioner for the "master race". When I saw DI French before embarking on my German adventure, he showed me some pieces of jewellery that had belonged to Frank. I think they were souvenirs, too, stolen from a man called SS-Sturmbannfuhrer Scharnhorst after Frank had murdered him.'

Lance Middleton sighed, and glanced at the kitchen clock.

'There's a train back to town at three fifteen,' he said, and Noel realized that their old friend was regaining some of his usual equanimity. They could now play out the ritual charade.

'Nonsense,' said Noel, 'you must join us for dinner and spend the night at my flat.'

'How very kind! In fact, I brought an overnight valise, just in case — but yes, how very kind! Chloe, might I trouble you for one last favour? I'd like to freshen up before dinner. If you'd point me in the direction of your bathroom . . .'

* * *

Over dinner, Lance began to pose some questions about the late Sir Frank Taylor, and what they should do about announcing their findings.

'As far as I see it, my friends,' said Lance, waving his fork in the air, 'there's no keeping his past crimes under wraps. Not anymore. I mean, for over seventy years, Franz Schneider was Frank Taylor, one of the crowning ornaments of the British stage. *For over seventy years.* At the moment, many people think that he might have been a Jewish refugee but nobody outside this room knows that he was once an SS guard. He was buried as Sir Frank Taylor. He has left considerable legacies that will bear his name. But his unspeakable past can't just be allowed to lie. Not with all the innocent lives he destroyed . . . the world deserves the full story. Starting with the police first thing tomorrow.'

Later that day, Noel drove Lance round to his side of Wellington Square and helped to settle him in the guest room. What an incredible man he was! His powers of investigation, and his training as a QC, made him a formidable opponent. Tomorrow morning, the three of them would present themselves at Jubilee House and lay all their findings before DI French and DS Edwards.

* * *

Paul French listened in silence while Lance told him and Glyn the truth about Sir Frank Taylor, alias Franz Schneider. Then he got up from his chair and stood at the window, looking down at the town hall car park. The others waited in silence for him to speak.

'Appalling,' he said at last. 'But from the police point of view, it doesn't help us much. It's the story of a dead man who never paid for his crimes, and in a manner of speaking lived so long that he had changed into a different person. Whether that story is ever made public is an entirely different matter. Nothing to do with us.'

'But don't you agree, sir, that it should be made public?' asked Glyn. 'The man was a war criminal who was never brought to justice. Why should he escape with his reputation intact?'

'That's not a police matter, Glyn. From our point of view, the interesting thing is that it lets us be a little more certain about who the assassin may have been. We can clear up one matter at once by telling Noel and Chloe about recent events here in Oldminster. A man called Josef Schmidt committed suicide in the block of flats where he lived, in Dover Street, by the canal. He left a note to say that he had failed in his mission to execute Frank Taylor for the murder of those two SS thugs that you mentioned by name in your story, Lance, SS-Sturmbannfuhrer Scharnhorst, and SS-Unterscharfuhrer Alois Schmidt. Josef Schmidt was Alois Schmidt's grandson.'

They were silent for a while, thinking of the murdered Unterscharfuhrer, who might have already had a wife and baby son waiting somewhere for him to return when the war ended. You try to define these Nazi criminals as though they were normal people, Noel Greenspan thought, but they were not, none of them. How many young men, women and babies had SS-Unterscharfuhrer Schmidt forced at bayonet point into the gas chambers?

'You see,' said Lance Middleton, 'the passage of time is so great here, seventy years, that we can't be speaking of people with common reactions to the atrocities of the Nazi era. People move on, children are born, and grandchildren, and new mindsets are developed. The victims, and the victims' descendants will never forget, and with rare exceptions, never forgive; but they no longer arrange their whole lives around the idea of quests for personal vengeance.'

'So what you're saying, Lance, is—'

'I'm saying that the people we are dealing with here, people like the man who committed suicide, are people suffering from psychiatric illnesses — monomania, the concept of the *idée fixe*.'

'That old man in the flats certainly fits the bill,' said DI French. 'He'd devoted his whole life to waiting to avenge the death of a distant forebear whom he'd never seen. A quest which led him to suicide.'

'So,' said DS Edwards, 'at first we thought that Sir Frank Taylor was a Jewish refugee. He'd been stabbed with an SS "honour dagger", and he had a letter warning him that someone was on the way to "extract vengeance". And when we look at Josef Schmidt, we find a man who had appointed himself "hereditary executioner", if you like. Not the executioner of an escaping Jewish prisoner, but of the SS guard who killed his senior officers. But the truth is, Josef Schmidt was an extreme individual, which is what Mr Middleton has suggested.'

'So you think—'

'I think, sir, there is more than one such extremist in this case. But to find them, we have to focus not on the history of Franz Schneider, but the murder of Sir Frank Taylor. His murderer is already here, in Oldminster, and has been for years — he's what they call a "sleeper", someone prepared to settle down beside his victim, and perhaps years later, choose the moment to strike. Do you remember that wreath of faded flowers that somebody brought to Sir Frank's funeral? It had the German word for "murderer" written on it.'

'DS Edwards and I both think we know who it was who murdered Sir Frank, and then added that sinister wreath to the others after his funeral. Glyn, tell them about Teddy Balonek.'

* * *

On Wednesday morning Glyn Edwards parked his police car in the road outside the Irving Home for Retired Actors, and made his way to the front door. There seemed to be nobody around, and it was some time before the door was answered. To his surprise, it was Tracey Potter who opened the door. She treated him to a shy smile and stood back to let him enter.

'Everybody's in the common room,' said Tracey, 'watching Mr Hayling's TV interview. It was amazing to see him actually on telly. He suddenly popped up on the screen, and I was like, Wow!'

It was, perhaps, typical of young Tracey that she didn't ask Glyn his business.

'What's Mr Hayling being interviewed about?'

'It's all about his adventures with the Kray twins. It's really cool, Mr Edwards.'

Glyn Edwards thought: *The Kray twins! Dear God, whatever will the man think up next?*

There was nobody in the kitchen, where the only sound was the murmur of the dishwasher. Should he risk a quick look in Teddy Balonek's room? He had no right to do so, but it was never a good idea to give a suspect any kind of advantage. He ran lightly up the stairs.

There was no need for him to open doors, because Teddy's room was clearly labelled *Teddy Balonek, Super-Chef* written in bold capital letters on a piece of card, and fixed to the door with now rusty drawing pins.

Glyn slipped into the room. Teddy's laptop stood open on a little shelf-like desk. Glyn froze at the sight of it, knowing that what he was contemplating was indefensible . . . But still he couldn't resist stepping forward, pressing the space bar. The screen flickered in to life. *Not even password protected.* Facing him was the unmistakeable image of a TOR browser, something that would keep Teddy's private internet surfing truly private. There were things that Teddy Balonek didn't want anyone to know about, things that stood out among the many raving lunacies of the internet as being particularly unsavoury, mad, and dangerous.

That was all he wanted to know. He knew now that Sir Frank Taylor had been a member of the SS, and that he had almost certainly been murdered in retaliation for his own killing spree among the Nazi faithful in his youth.

He was convinced that the only person who could have committed the murder was somebody who actually lived in the main building of the Irving Home, and who could creep downstairs unseen from his upstairs flat. The time had come to confront Teddy Balonek.

When Glyn returned to the kitchen, he found that Balonek was already there. Clad in his chef's whites, he stood by one of the ovens, near to a rack of fearsome looking knives. He stood quite still, supporting himself by leaning against one of the marble-topped counters.

'Tracey told me that you'd called,' he said, 'so I thought I'd come here now to see what you wanted.' He picked up one of the fearsome knives, looked closely at the blade, and returned it to its rack. 'But in fact,' he said, 'I know what you want, so I'll save us both time by making my confession.'

They stood on either side of the big, scrubbed kitchen table, and both could feel the tension in the air. The dishwasher still murmured away, and the kitchen clock seemed to be ticking more loudly than usual.

'You confess to the murder of Sir Frank Taylor?'

He had made the mistake of moving away from the door, which was the only exit. Balonek still stood perilously near the fearsome knives. Glyn wished that he had brought another copper with him. Balonek's reply, when it came, was totally unexpected.

'Confess to the murder? Don't be so bloody daft! I want to confess that I told you a lie when I said that my grandfather served in the Polish Free Forces. In fact, he was a police inspector in the Polish Criminal Police—'

'Yes, Teddy, I know he was,' said Glyn, sighing with relief. He sat down at the table. 'I found out all about your grandfather's career by exercising what you might call my detective skills. You can see, can't you, that it made you a suspicious character? But I'm very relieved to hear you deny that you murdered Sir Frank Taylor, and I'll tell you at once that I believe you. Did you know who Sir Frank really was?'

'Yes, I knew who he was. And I knew that there were certain people who were out for his blood. It was my grandfather who investigated the murders of those two SS men — Scharnhorst and Schmidt. They may have been war criminals, but they were murdered, and my grandfather was a good police officer, who assembled enough circumstantial evidence to show that Franz Schneider had committed those crimes.'

Teddy Balonek opened the oven door and brought out a plate covered with a saucer. 'I prepared this as a peace offering,' he said. 'I cooked it while you were nosing around in my room upstairs.'

DS Edwards had the grace to blush as Teddy presented him with a very substantial bacon sandwich.

'You view sensitive material on your computer,' he said, biting into the sandwich.

'Oh, so you saw the Tor browser?' said Teddy. 'I follow a few so-called far-right political sites in Poland. They're not yet proscribed, but they may be, one day. They're mainly sites dedicated to the restoration of the Polish monarchy. Some of them are quite touching. Others are just run by nutters.'

'Polish monarchy? I didn't know there'd ever been a Polish monarchy.'

'Well, there was. But get this, Sergeant. I've a keen interest in Polish history. I regarded Sir Frank as a — as a historical curiosity, if you like, who had morphed into an old, frail man who lived with us here at the Irving Home. And that's all.'

'You had two German newspapers, which you threw away, pretending that they belonged to Sir Frank Taylor.'

'True. How did you know that?'

'Somebody saw you,' Glyn said dismissively. 'Why did you throw them away?'

'I was expecting us all to be searched. I occasionally buy a German daily paper. The other one was a souvenir, which contained the announcement of my grandfather's acceptance into the Polish Criminal Police.'

'I can get that back for you, if you like,' said Glyn. 'Why did you decide to confess to lying about your grandfather?'

'Because Father Randall at St Anthony's advised me to. Any more questions?'

'Yes. Is there any chance of a cup of tea?'

16. WHAT HAPPENED TO BOSSZUALLO

Clive Martin was nineteen years old, with his fortune to make. He considered himself lucky that Mr Sanders had agreed to employ him as his front-of-shop assistant at the Old Curiosity Shop. Mr Sanders was a pleasant, kindly man, though he could have his moods! Clive believed in being at work well before they opened for business, so he always caught the 17c bus from Riverside, and got off at Cathedral Green.

It was a quarter to nine when he turned the corner into Provost's Lane. It was a bright, pleasant morning, with a clear blue sky above. There was Mr Sanders' Bentley, parked in the unnamed alley beside the shop. At the beginning of the year Mr Sanders had given him a key to the front door, a sure sign that he was fully accepted as a member of the team — well, at least, as a trusted assistant. There would have to be more than two of them to qualify as a team.

But what was this? The door was open. It wasn't like Mr Sanders to leave the place unlocked overnight. Inside, everything was quiet. He stood for a moment, listening to the ticking of the various clocks clamouring to be bought. The lights were not on.

'Mr Sanders?'

No reply. Maybe he was ill. He'd been to the doctor's several times recently. Mr Sanders lived in an apartment above the shop, a fascinating place, with shelves full of antique books, several China cabinets, and a silk-covered sofa which Mr Sanders had told him once belonged to Madame Récamier. Clive had promised himself to find out who she was, but hadn't yet got round to doing so.

He went into the little galley kitchen behind the shop, filled the electric kettle, and turned it on. He'd better go upstairs and see was there any sign of Mr Sanders.

Minutes later, the other shopkeepers in the little court off Provost's Lane saw the frantic youth dash out from the front door of the Old Curiosity Shop, shouting 'Murder! Murder!' to the clear blue sky.

* * *

DI French climbed the stairs that led from Mervyn Sanders' shop to his flat on the first floor. A police car had managed to park in the small common courtyard.

When he entered the bedroom, French saw Ray Dunwoody kneeling beside an inert, bloodstained figure lying on the floor beside a glass-fronted bookcase that appeared to have been sprayed with droplets of fresh blood. A uniformed police constable stood by the window. Almost without thinking, DI French asked his by now ritual question.

'What have you got for me?'

'I've met Mervyn Sanders,' said French, still looking around the room in puzzlement. 'It was he who confirmed that the dagger used to kill Sir Frank Taylor was the genuine article. I'm sorry he's dead.'

'He isn't. That's what I've been trying to tell you. There was a mix-up — the lad who found the body was in such a state they didn't know who to send. I was passing and heard the fuss on the radio so I came straight up. It's lucky I did. This isn't Mervyn Sanders lying here,' said Dr Dunwoody, 'this is Charles Forshaw, one of the retired actors from the

Irving Home. And he isn't dead, but he will be if that ambulance doesn't arrive soon — Ah! I can hear it now.'

Paul French was battling with disbelief. He'd expected to see the dead body of Mervyn Sanders, and that was what he *had* seen — a bloodstained body, the face turned away from him towards the wall. But when he looked now, he saw that it was indeed Charles Forshaw. He heard the shop door flung open, and heavy purposeful feet climbing the stairs.

Dr Dunwoody stood up.

'I'm going with him in the ambulance,' he said. 'He suffered a massive blow to the front of the skull, inflicted by that brass statuette lying on the floor behind the door. A statuette of the god Pan, part human, part goat. It's not a very heavy thing, as you can see, but it was used with force.'

'Will he survive?'

'It's touch and go . . .' He stopped speaking as the paramedics came into the room.

DI French retreated downstairs to the little kitchen at the back of the shop, and phoned Glyn. He wasn't on duty till ten, but he'd want to be in on this from the start. Charles Forshaw! French made an effort to control a rising anger. This case, with its roots in Nazism, seemed to be casting a baleful shadow over the whole town.

* * *

PC George Steele had always been content with his rank. He knew that he was a plodder, and that he'd never make it to sergeant. Early on in his career he'd sat the sergeants' examination and failed. His inspector in those days had advised him not to bother in future. 'You're a good man-on-the-beat, Steele,' he'd said. 'There's a crying need for men like you in the Force.' And so he'd plodded on, happy with his lot.

Today, his morning duty took him to Gladstone Park, where he'd do a gentle patrol, while admiring the floral displays for which the Oldminster Parks Department was renowned. You could smell the spring in the air. He stopped

166

to admire the floral clock, and then continued his beat along the central drive.

He stopped when he saw a well-dressed gentleman sitting on a park bench. He was talking to himself and wringing his hands. His face, shirt and jacket were covered in blood.

'Good morning, sir,' said PC Steele. 'It's a lovely day for May.'

'It is,' said the bloodstained man, 'but I wouldn't be surprised if we had rain later. My name's Sanders, by the way. Mervyn Sanders.'

'And I'm PC George Steele, sir. Pleased to meet you.'

'Likewise,' said Mervyn Sanders, and offered Steele a blood-covered hand to shake.

'It's been a long, long, journey, officer,' said Sanders, 'a journey that has taken me along many dark and dangerous paths. I'm of Hungarian origin, you know, which is why I took the name Bosszuallo for trawling the web. It's Hungarian for "Avenger". "Vengeance is mine, I will repay, says the Lord." But He needs human hands to carry out His vengeance. Did you know that Hungarian and Finnish are closely related languages? Not many people are aware of that.'

PC Steele sat down on the bench beside Mervyn Sanders.

'If you don't mind, sir,' he said, 'I'll call through to headquarters to send someone out here who can help you.'

'That's very kind of you, Mr Steele. May I call you George?'

'"George" will do very nicely, sir.' PC Steele began to talk quietly into his TETRA radio as Sanders continued to ramble on.

'I was the designated Avenger for my mother's kindred, you see. Did I mention that my mother was Polish? Her family moved to Germany over a hundred years ago, and they regarded themselves as German. German Jews, you know. I received help and support from another Avenger, a man called Msciciel, which means Avenger in Polish. We communicated regularly.

'I thought I'd done it very cleverly — making away with Franz Schneider, you know. But then, *he* turned up at my shop this morning, and told me that the game was up. Sometimes, I seem to be two persons, struggling against each other. Split personality. I saw a doctor in Chichester, who said that my personality was disintegrating. Quite frankly I was terrified. I never went back to see him. What's happening to me? It's been getting worse for months.'

'And this man who came to see you this morning, sir. What kind of a man was he?'

'He was one of those actors who live at the Irving Home. Charles Forshaw. I'd met him before, when I bought a few things from him. He seemed to be quite a nice sort of person. But this morning, when he was talking to me, I could see the Devil looking out of his eyes, and a voice in my head warned me that I was in mortal danger. So I killed him. Killed the Devil, you understand.'

PC Steele was thankful at that moment for his stolid, undramatic approach to things. If necessary, he would sit on that bench all morning, until back-up arrived.

'And what was it that this Charles Forshaw claimed to know?'

'Well, he saw how I had contrived to execute Franz Schneider during the night of 20 April. Only Satan could have told him how I did it.'

Two police cars appeared at the far end of the drive, moving slowly towards them as they sat together on the bench.

'I have terrible headaches, George,' said Mervyn Sanders. 'Maybe they will go, now that I've explained things to you. Hungarian and Finnish form a little language group of their own. We're open from nine to five, closed Saturday morning. You'd be welcome any time that you wanted to look round. I suppose I'll be hanged?'

'No, sir,' said George Steele. 'You won't be hanged. That went out years ago.'

He saw Mervyn Sanders safely into one of the police cars, nodded to the police officers who had come in answer to his call, and then resumed his patrol of Gladstone Park.

* * *

'He will look quite normal to you,' said Dr Klein, the duty psychiatrist at Oakvale House, a psychiatric unit not far from Oldminster, 'because he is heavily medicated, so that the more dominant of his two personalities is in control at the moment.'

'That personality being—'

'The well-regarded antique dealer and solid citizen, who until recently had never fallen foul of the law in his whole life. But you will realize, Inspector French, that Mervyn Sanders has been diagnosed as suffering from acute schizophrenia, a condition in which illusion and reality cannot always be differentiated. Part of him is an amiable, docile, man, quite kindly in his dealings with others, the other part is that of a being consumed by monomania, a being who is a ruthless avenger of specific wrongs.'

The doctor was a quietly spoken, rather prim man in his forties. He spoke clearly and calmly as they paced down the white, clinical corridors of the centre.

'But Sergeant Edwards and I will be able to have a normal conversation with him?'

'Yes, indeed. But you will find that his moral integrity has disintegrated — he no longer understands the broad differences between right and wrong. He has readily admitted that he murdered Sir Frank Taylor, describing his cold rage and lack of pity while he did so. While in that personality he was the Avenger; only after he had done the deed, did he revert to Mervyn Sanders the antique dealer.'

'When he attacked Mr Charles Forshaw,' said DI French, 'was he the Avenger then? Mr Forshaw had never done him any harm.'

'Forshaw came to see him in his flat above the shop, very early in the morning, and told him that he knew how he had committed the murder of Sir Frank Taylor. That statement triggered what we call a psychotic episode, an extremely dangerous incident that brought the obsessive Avenger to the fore. Sanders projected his own guilty persona on to that of Charles Forshaw. He said he saw the Devil dancing in Forshaw's eyes and killed him.'

They'd reached a room near the end of a corridor, and the doctor tapped on the door. It was immediately opened by a very tall man in a white jacket and trousers, who stood aside to let them enter.

Mervyn Sanders was sitting at a table, leafing through the pages of a motoring magazine. The white walls of the room held framed pastel studies of birds and plants. A rather dismal rubber-plant in a tub filled one corner of the room.

Mervyn got up from the table and smiled a welcome.

'Inspector French and Sergeant Edwards, how nice to see you both again! My offer of £500 for the Nazi dagger is still open, you know. It was there lying to hand when I entered Franz Schneider's room, and it seemed almost providential that he should be executed with one of the vile weapons of his own beloved SS.'

'How are you, Mr Sanders?' asked DI French. 'Do you feel any better, now?'

'I feel very much better thank you — more myself, if you know what I mean. They are very kind here. Particularly Dr Klein.' He gave a funny little bow to the doctor. 'My only regret is that I am going to be hanged for killing that very nice man, Charles Forshaw. I bought some things from him, you know — some nice pieces. I was so sorry when he came to my flat and drove me out of my senses.'

'Mr Forshaw isn't dead,' DI French began, but stopped speaking at a sign from Dr Klein.

'Oh yes, I'm afraid he's dead, and so I must pay the supreme penalty. I'm sorry about Forshaw, but I'm glad I was able to avenge my mother's family at long last. They came from Mannheim, you know, where their family had lived for more than a century. Obviously, I was too young to have known any of them, but my own family — the Sanders — always had long memories. I lost all my European kin in Hungary: they were all transported to Auschwitz.

'My mother's family were called Shapiro, and they lived in Mannheim, a pleasant town in Baden-Wurttemberg. Alphonse was a timber exporter, and he lived with his wife

Anne, and his son, Chaim Jakob. Anne came from an academic Jewish family, the Goldbergs, and my mother's family were descended from Anne's sister, Sophie, who sought refuge in Sweden, thus escaping the Holocaust.

'Well, the Shapiros were all rounded up and sent to the Stutthof concentration camp, twenty-one miles east of what was then called Danzig. They were gassed days after they arrived in the camp, but from the time of their arrival until the day of their death, they were terrorized by Franz Schneider, the man who would become the great British actor, Sir Frank Taylor. We were told that detail about Schneider by some people who survived that camp, and whose stories were available in Polish on the internet. I was chosen a long time ago to carry out the death sentence on Franz Schneider.'

'Chosen, Mr Sanders? Who was it who chose you?' asked French.

'No one knows who controls the organization that seeks out Nazi criminals for execution, but they are readily available for consultation on what some people fancifully call the Dark Net. They have no connection with the Wiesenthal organization, or the State of Israel.'

DS Edwards thought: Can this man really be mad? We are holding a civilized conversation here, and Mr Sanders is giving a sober and *almost* coherent account of what happened to the Shapiro family, his mother's murdered kindred.

'That is a terrible story that you've told us, Mr Sanders,' he said.

'It is, indeed. And Stutthof was a terrible place. Who can say what became of Chaim Jakob after he ended up there?'

'And you murdered Sir Frank Taylor?' asked DI French.

'I did. Except that I don't see it as murder. God sent me to wreak His vengeance on him.'

'How did you contrive to get into the Irving Home to carry out your "execution"?'

Mervyn Sanders laughed, and shook a finger at the inspector.

'No, no, I'm not telling you how I did that! That will be my secret! Maybe I used magic, or necromancy, rendering myself invisible. But you'll never know. Forshaw said that he knew, but Forshaw is dead. Is that the time? I really must be getting back to the shop, now. Clive will be getting worried.'

A sign from the doctor told both detectives that it was time to leave.

'Goodbye, Inspector, and you, Sergeant Edwards. It's been very nice talking to you. I should like a rabbi to be present at my execution, which will take place on the thirty-first of this month, which will be a Thursday, thus avoiding any profanation of the Sabbath.'

It felt both bizarre and yet perfectly natural to shake hands with Mervyn Sanders before he was led away by the burly warder.

'What will happen to him, Doctor?' asked DI French.

'If our advice is taken, he will not be brought to trial — he is utterly unfit to plead, as you have seen. My colleagues and I feel quite certain that early next month he will be committed to Broadmoor.'

* * *

'Broadmoor? Oh dear, what a tragedy. I blame myself.'

When the two detectives returned from Oakvale House, they found Rabbi Hertzberg of Pitt Street Synagogue waiting for them. A small, full-bearded man, his normally cheerful face was shadowed by shock and worry.

'Why do you say that, Dr Hertzberg?' asked DI French.

'He came to me,' said the rabbi, 'full of concern for his mental state. He only came occasionally to the synagogue services, but he was an observant Jew, after his fashion. Well, he came to see me one evening in Pitt Street, and told me that he was becoming mentally disturbed. He said that he had had frightful thoughts and urges for many years, but while his parents were alive, he was able to control these urges. I knew them both, they were devout, but practical folk — down-to-earth, you know. Once they had gone, Mervyn Sanders was left exposed to whatever demons were haunting him.'

172

'What did you do?'

'I recommended he visited a very clever Jungian psychiatrist who has a practice in Chichester. He went there, but became agitated, and left. The psychiatrist got in touch with me and urged me to have another go at persuading Mervyn to return to his clinic, but I never did. I got immersed in other matters, and when I caught glimpses of Mervyn in town, he seemed to be his old self again.'

'You've nothing to reproach yourself with, Dr Hertzberg,' said DI French. 'I don't think Mervyn Sanders has been his "old self" for half a lifetime.'

Rabbi Hertzberg nodded sadly.

'He has a sister, Elizabeth, who lives in South Shields with her husband. She married out of the faith, and the family disowned her. Mervyn had all but forgotten her existence, but she sends me the occasional postcard. I must let her know what has happened to her brother.'

'Sir,' said Glyn Edwards when the rabbi had left them, 'I wouldn't feel too sorry for Sanders, if I were you. After all, he did murder Sir Frank Taylor, and almost did for poor Mr Forshaw, as well. I like that man. I think he's a first-rate bloke. Do we know whether he'll survive that attack?'

'He's in the intensive care unit at the Princess Diana Hospital. One of the doctors phoned me to say that he's in an induced coma, but they're hopeful that he's going to make it. Apparently, despite his age, he's in good physical condition. All we can do, Glyn, is hope and pray.'

* * *

Noel Greenspan, Chloe McArthur and Lance Middleton were lingering over coffee in the kitchen of Chloe's flat in Wellington Square. It was three days after Mervyn Sanders' assault on Charles Forshaw. They had eaten what Chloe termed a 'modest' dinner, consisting of a chicken Provencal with olives and artichokes, followed by a summer pudding.

'It's a bit like the funeral baked meats,' said Chloe. 'We've nothing to celebrate, have we? Poor Charles Forshaw was our client, acting on behalf of the late Sir Frank Taylor, and all of us were going after the wrong man, leaving Mervyn Sanders to murder poor Charles. It is murder, isn't it? Mr Forshaw is not going to survive that attack.'

'You're wrong there, Chloe,' said Lance. 'I have a good friend at the Princess Diana Hospital, a surgeon, who was able to tell me a few things in confidence. I phoned him yesterday from London, and what he told me brought me down here to see you both.'

'If it's good news you're bringing,' said Chloe, 'you should have told us as soon as you came, and then we wouldn't have had to sit round looking miserable all through dinner. What did your surgeon friend tell you?'

'I apologize for not having told you sooner,' said Lance, 'but you know what I'm like — a repository of secrets which I bring to the light of day when I think the moment is right.'

'If you don't tell us what you know about Charles Forshaw,' said Noel, 'I may resort to violence. Tell us, will you? And no shilly-shallying.'

'The frontal bone of Forshaw's skull was fractured in three places, with one bone fragment detached from the rest of the skull. They put him into a coma, and operated on him on Thursday evening, and to everybody's relief ascertained that his brain had sustained only slight bruising. None of his intellectual faculties will be impaired. They intend to insert a silver plate into his skull, thus restoring and strengthening the whole frontal area. There will be some scarring, my friend says, but nothing much out of the ordinary. And he *will* recover, Chloe, I've been assured of that.'

'How did you come to know a surgeon at the Princess Diana? You're a London-based man.'

'I am well known for my contacts,' said Lance. He contrived to look modest, but failed. 'You know, when I asked you that time whether the truth about Sir Frank Taylor should be made public, I half hoped that you'd agree to keep the whole thing quiet. But I'm glad, now, that you gave the verdict that you did. There had been too many deeply hidden secrets, and it was time for the truth to be told.'

He added, inconsequentially, 'There's something rather distinguished about having a silver plate inserted into your head.'

'There is something that we *can* celebrate this evening,' said Noel, 'and that's your willingness to fly to Germany at a moment's notice, and to extract so much information there about Franz Schneider, and the doomed Shapiro family. Without your input, I don't suppose we'd ever have found out the truth.'

Lance Middleton looked pleased but was in no mood for preening.

'Of all the details of my European trip,' he said, 'one thing has stuck in my memory. It was old Brother Anselm's description of the bleak room with the doors for ever blowing open, and the floor awash with water, into which all the precious documents of whole families had been thrown and trodden underfoot. Among those documents was the blood-stained passport that had belonged to young Chaim Jakob Shapiro, used by Franz Schneider to make his escape to the British Zone, while its rightful owner had been reduced to anonymous ashes, together with his parents.'

Lance's normally placid face suddenly flushed with anger.

'I'm glad Sir Frank Taylor is dead,' he said. 'I'm glad that old man in the flats is dead. I'm glad that Mervyn Sanders will be sent to a place where he'll not be able to harm anyone else.'

They had been drinking a sweet white wine with their dessert, and Lance refilled their glasses. They knew what he was going to do, and stood up at the table.

'My friends,' said Lance Middleton, 'I give you a toast. To the memory of Chaim Jakob Shapiro and his parents.'

They repeated his words and raised their glasses in solemn tribute.

EPILOGUE

Detective Sergeant Edwards joined the solemn procession along the stone-flagged passage of the prison. It was a grim, colourless place, and he felt that he was acting in a long-forgotten black-and-white film. Their boots resounded on the flags. Why was it so cold? After all, it was May, not the depth of winter.

The stern, bearded man leading them was probably the governor. A clergyman walked behind him, clad in cassock and surplice, reading aloud from a book of prayers. 'I am the Resurrection and the Life,' he said. The prisoner, chained hand and foot, and supported by two impassive warders, made no reply.

A door ahead of them was opened, and Glyn could see the gallows, and the waiting hangman. He thought: This can't be happening. But it was . . . 'It'll all be over in a minute,' said the governor. 'Sergeant Edwards, would you care to assist the hangman?'

Glyn jerked awake and sat up in bed, his heart pounding, the governor's words still echoing in his ears. The duvet lay in a heap beside the bed. That would account for the feeling of cold in the dream.

Since his heart-to-heart talk with Sandra, he had started to take more care of himself. Part of that care was to cook himself a decent breakfast, rather than lie too long in bed in the morning, feeling sorry for himself. He made himself some bacon and eggs, and sat down with a mug of tea at the kitchen table. The house smelled of fresh paint and the clean, satisfying scent of drying wallpaper. What day was it? Thursday, 31 May. Somebody had mentioned that date recently. Something to do with work, no doubt. Inspector French would know.

Sandra was coming home at the end of next week, and she would not be the Sandra who had been forced to lie about visiting her mother in order to seek the help she'd so desperately needed. He had no doubts at all in his mind that when she walked through the front door it would be as the mistress not only of her own house, but of her own destiny.

He finished his breakfast and washed up the plates. It was ten past eight, time to get out to Jubilee House. He had just opened the front door when the phone rang. It was Inspector French. Mervyn Sanders had been found hanged in his cell at Oakvale House. He had fashioned a noose from a bed sheet. He had left a note, saying that he had been ordered to make away with himself by the dark voices whispering inside his head.

It was then that Glyn remembered some words that Mervyn Sanders had spoken when he and Mr French were interviewing him. 'I should like a rabbi to be present at my execution, which will take place on the thirty-first of this month, which will be a Thursday, thus avoiding any prof-anation of the Sabbath.' Nobody had thought to listen to a madman. What a world this was! What a thorough waste, all round! There had been no rabbi present at Mervyn Sanders' 'execution'.

* * *

A judicial inquiry into the death of Mervyn Sanders in the secure facility known as Oakvale House was held at the end of June. Dr Robert Klein, director of the facility, declared that the patient had shown no obvious signs of suicidal tendency, and had seemed content to cooperate in every way with the medical staff. He had been placed on a regime of medication designed, among other things, to render him docile, and it had come as a shock when he had been discovered hanged in his cell. Since then, more robust measures had been put in place to ensure that nothing of a like nature would occur in the future. The inquiry found that no blame attached to Oakvale House and its personnel, and agreed with the coroner's verdict of 'suicide while the balance of the mind was disturbed'.

* * *

In the second week of July DI French learned from an NHS consultant friend that Charles Forshaw had been released from the Princess Diana Hospital, and was back in the Irving Home for Retired Actors.

'I think we should call on him, Glyn,' he said, 'and see for ourselves how he is. I'll phone Nurse Trickett and arrange for us to be invited to visit him.'

'That would be nice, sir. But you've got a specific reason for wanting to see him, haven't you?'

DI French laughed.

'Yes, I have. I want to know how on earth Charles Forshaw realized that it was Mervyn Sanders who had murdered Sir Frank Taylor.'

'The press made mincemeat of Sir Frank,' said Glyn Edwards.

The *Daily Telegraph* had launched its own investigation, with harrowing pictures of concentration camp victims, and photographs of swaggering SS men rounding up innocent people. They even managed to find some pre-war photographs of the Shapiro family — not the ones the police had on file — and reproduced them. By the time they'd finished, Frank Taylor's life and reputation were in tatters.

'The *Telegraph*'s letters pages were full of demands for Frank to be posthumously deprived of his knighthood,' said

DI French. 'But the upshot of it all is that Frank Taylor is now *persona non grata*. The Dean of Oldminster is proposing that his grave in the churchyard should be left unmarked.'

'Well, sir,' said DS Edwards with a sigh, 'it's all over and done with. So let's tie up that loose end by asking Charles Forshaw how he knew that Mervyn Sanders had committed murder.'

* * *

They were both surprised how well Charles Forshaw looked. They found him sitting in the common room, reading that morning's edition of the *Oldminster Gazette*. He broke into a smile as they entered the room and rose to greet them. His handsome face was a little thinner than they remembered, and his hair had been restyled to mask most of the scar tissue on his forehead.

'How kind of you both to come and see me,' he said, resuming his seat. 'Yes, I'm fine, really, apart from the occasional headache.' He laughed. 'Teddy Balonek told me that you thought *he*'d done it, Sergeant Edwards — oh, there's no need to blush! But no, it wasn't him. I was sitting here in this room one day in May, when it suddenly came to me who must have murdered old Frank.'

He frowned, and became lost in thought. DI French gently brought him back to the present.

'And how did you realize that, Mr Forshaw?' he asked.

'Well, you see, I knew that nobody here at the Irving Home could have done it. It would have been nonsense to think otherwise. But on that dreadful night, the twentieth of April, there was another man here, a stranger in our midst. Mervyn Sanders, to whom I'd sold some pieces of silver, was here giving us a lecture on the fate of the Russian Crown Jewels. Very interesting it was, too. He got here about seven, and was met by Trudy Vosper at reception. She'd stayed on especially to book him in. We all had dinner, and then he gave his talk.

179

'He left at ten o'clock, long after Trudy had gone home, and we heard the front door slam as he went out. At least, that's what we thought we heard. But it wasn't so.'

Forshaw got up from his chair and led them out into the passage leading off the entrance hall. He pointed to two large wardrobes built into the passage wall.

'What he did, gentlemen, was slam the front door, and then hurry back and hide in one of these wardrobes. There's plenty of room in either of them for a man to stand. Tony and I were with Frank in the common room until eleven or so. When all was quiet, and presumably far into the night, Sanders came out, stole into Frank's room, did the deed, and returned to the wardrobe, where he would have stayed until Gareth Pugh the handyman came in at seven thirty. It would have been desperately uncomfortable, but when you've just committed murder, I don't suppose you'd be very choosy. Once the alarms were switched off, and the front door open, he slipped out unnoticed, and got clean away.'

'What about the CCTV? We examined that, you know, and saw no sign of anyone entering or leaving the building that night.'

'Well, Inspector, isn't that precisely the problem? You should have seen him leaving, but I was so convinced he'd left that I suppose I convinced you too. As it is, our CCTV camera doesn't point directly at the door — it's angled to take in the faces of people coming out. So you wouldn't have seen him standing at the door talking to me, nor going back inside and slamming it shut behind him. And he'd taken a taxi to the house, so nobody would have seen his car parked out there overnight.

'Sanders arrived here before the CCTV was turned on for the night, and then he left after Gareth Pugh had turned off the CCTV in the morning to extract the night-tape. I think Sanders was lucky not to be seen, because of course he couldn't have had any knowledge of our security arrangements.' He added, wryly, 'I was about to say, "the Devil looks after his own", but perhaps I shouldn't.

'Anyway, I thought about the matter for a long time, and in the end foolishly decided to confront Sanders myself, instead of informing you of my suspicions. I went to his shop on the twenty-fourth of May, and — well, you know what happened then.'

Charles Forshaw stood up. He looked tired and strained.

'Well, gentlemen,' he said, 'time for me to take a nap. We all continue to creak along quite well, here. We've a new man coming soon, another stalwart of television in the seventies, to fill the place left vacant by Frank Taylor. I sincerely hope that he'll have a happy and mercifully uneventful time here with us, at the Irving Home for Retired Actors.'

THE END

ALSO BY NORMAN RUSSELL

THE OLDMINSTER MYSTERIES
Book 1: AN INVITATION TO MURDER
Book 2: AN ANTIQUE MURDER

Made in United States
North Haven, CT
08 August 2022

22418045R00114